The
Beautiful Friend

and other stories

Other Books by Mary Stolz

The
Beautiful Friend

and other stories

by Mary Stolz

Harper & Brothers | *Publishers* New York

33 871

To

Betty Jo Ramsey

Contents

The
Beautiful Friend

and other stories

The
Beautiful Friend

I'm one of those plain girls with charm and a beautiful friend. It is not an unusual combination. Beautiful girls don't ordinarily flock together, for fear of getting in one another's way, I suppose. On the other hand, they don't want to run around with social liabilities. This is how people like Mady and me begin acquaintances that often become friendships. Ours did.

I have no more of an inferiority complex than is consistent with not having beauty in a world that just adores it. I do have charm. People besides my relatives think so. Sometimes even I think so. Charm, I believe, is a matter of making the most of your natural advantages, and liking people. I do these—the first with some effort, the second with almost none. Still, I'm a realist (even if Michael does call me a romantic) and I know plain when I see and live with it every day. For years it didn't bother me, anyway not morbidly. It was just something I knew, like the multiplication table. Multiplication isn't the cheeriest thing in the world, but it's nothing to brood over. That's what I told myself, until I met Michael.

The Beautiful Friend

Only that's getting ahead of my story.

Mady Tyrone and I met in boarding school. Though we'd lived in the same house for a couple of years and knew each other to speak to, even enough to sit down now and then and talk together, we weren't actually friends. Our lives and our aims were too dissimilar. Mady was a skimmer. She ran over the surface of life like a bright insect over the surface of a brook, humming, darting, taking no thought for the morrow. I didn't skim. I walked along, one charming foot in front of the other, knowing where I was, where I'd been, and generally trying too hard to figure out where I was going.

So there was no reason for Mady and me to improve upon our vaguely pleasant acquaintance. But in our third year she got campused for three months for dancing cheek to cheek with a boy from Choate. I ran into her a few minutes after she'd received this sentence. She was idling along toward the house, an expression on her face that was half vexed, half amused.

"Oh, hi, Ella," she said, and as we walked together, added, "You know, the only difference between this place and a girls' correction school is that our parents pay for us to get repressed and overdisciplined."

"What happened to you?"

When she told me, I burst out laughing. "Sorry," I said, after a bit, "but it's just so . . . so archaic. What period of the world's history do they think we're living in?"

She looked at me oddly and smiled. "That's practically

what I said. I mean, I think I'd have gotten away with only a month, but I asked why we didn't act in a really consistent fashion and revive the minuet. That did it."

From then on we saw quite a bit of each other, and Mady actually wasn't too put out about her three months of restriction. She brought up her grades for a while and sewed slip straps and things. For a girl like Mady a few weeks without dates constituted a vacation. She got restless toward the end, of course, but on the whole we enjoyed it. And then when she burst upon society anew, she took me along with her.

I never pretended to myself that I'd have had the fun of that last year and a half without Mady's sponsorship. On the other hand, the boys I knew and went out with may have started it for Mady's sake, or with the idea that they could get to her through me, but most of them ended up liking me for myself alone. (There's that charm.) Well . . . a good many of them. I'm pretty sure. (There's the inferiority complex.) The thing is that until I met Michael no man's feelings toward me were important enough for me to wonder long or care deeply as to how much was calculation and how much true affection.

I had fun and grew, not pretty, but less plain. It's a side effect of happiness, and any girl would be happy to lead the sort of life I led then. I was, quite consciously, grateful to Mady. And, in other ways, for other reasons, she was to me. She said I gave her a sense of reality, and I know I helped her pass English and French. That pleased her parents, and Mady liked to please her parents, and . . . oh, there are wheels within wheels and all sorts of reasons why people become friends and all sorts of ways in which they affect each other.

So, thanks to the indecorous boy from Choate, I left boarding school with some notion of skimming and the realization that it could be fun. Mady left it less heedless and slightly more willing to face the fact that there is a tomorrow. I would say we both gained.

Mady went to Bennington, then, to study art. I went to Radcliffe and majored in English literature. My father is a professor at M.I.T., so I could live at home, which I liked. There were still dates and dancing and I had friends besides Mady. It wasn't the same, but somehow that year and a half of whirl was like an interlude to me, essentially not the whirling type. Mady and I corresponded. Sometimes she came to Boston with her parents and would leave them to stay with me. She was certainly still whirling . . . from one man to another to another. Mady had never done anything so pedestrian as to go steady, and while girls around her got married and left school, or got married and stayed, or became engaged and began to take life seriously, Mady danced.

Then in my senior year I met Michael. He was a graduate student doing chemical research and my father had spoken several times of "young Farquhar" with high approval, but I had never met him, nor expected to, nor wished to. So far as I could make out from my admittedly preoccupied father, young Farquhar was all work and no play. Association with Mady had ruined me for the type.

On a gingery fall evening just before dark, Dad came in the front door, saying over his shoulder, "Come on in, Michael. I have the papers in my study. . . . Oh, hello, Ella dear." He turned toward the living room, where I was sprawled in something unglamorous reading Boswell. I glanced up from the pages, intending to greet Dad and glance right back again, and there was Michael.

All work and no play *indeed,* I thought, and gave my father a reproachful glance which he didn't notice.

Michael didn't look as if he did research. He looked as if he rode out on sunny afternoons to joust with the king. He looked as if he swam in tropical seas, picking up doubloons from the ocean floor and swapping tales of privateers with the ghost of Captain Kidd. His eyes were full of challenge and curiosity, as a researcher's should be, but they had something else. A glint that another century would have called high-mettled. I looked at him and wished I had spun-gold hair down to my feet and a wall of briers in front of me that he could hack his way through. I wished I were wearing ruby velvet with lace at the wrists and stood in some high Renaissance peril, so that he could ride to my rescue.

I wished, with all my heart, for the first time in my life, that I were beautiful.

I put Boswell aside, tried to tuck my shirttail in, wondered if I'd eaten off my lipstick, and got up. "Hi, Dad," I said, and the Renaissance went glimmering.

"Ella, this is Michael Farquhar. My daughter, Michael."

He did not say, "Ella, here is your fate," and they, intent on papers in the study, didn't know. But I knew.

I didn't see him after that for over two weeks. Apparently there was nothing further in Dad's study—and nothing in Dad's house—to draw him back again. But on a still, chill, metallic afternoon I ran into him near the Fogg Museum, and he knew me immediately. He said, "Hello, Miss Morrison," and I sighed and said, "Hello."

Clutching my books, my mind dreams and years ahead of his, I smiled up at him. If I can marry you, I thought, I'm going to. I didn't think there might be another girl, that he might already be married. I didn't feel predatory, nor in the least ashamed. I simply felt what I had to feel, that I had found my love in this man, and that if—by art or intellect—I could win him, I would.

"Are you on your way in or out?" he asked, indicating the museum.

"Oh . . . either," I said, and he smiled.

"Then let's go get a cup of coffee."

"Yes, let's," I breathed, and we fell into step together.

That's as good a way as any to put it. We fell into step together. And after a few weeks Michael fell in love with me, and we were together in that, too.

There wasn't any other girl. I found, during our talks, our walks, our evenings in the library at home, and—occasionally—a concert or a dinner downtown, that he hadn't taken a girl out since his undergraduate days. Michael was terribly busy. Perilously close to being all work and no play, after all. He was, as the best scientists are, dedicated to science. Love me as he did—and he did —he still had little time for concerts or dinners downtown or evenings of talk. He didn't, to put it another way, have much time for me. But I understood about that. I'd grown up in a house with another dedicated scientist. And the time he did have for me was so completely, so beautifully, mine. It's a way Michael has, and I think it's rare, of being able to give himself to the moment.

Oh, but those were beautiful weeks, with winter coming on, and the snow-heavy sky closing in, and the firelight on Michael's face when we sat together on the library sofa near the hearth, talking of everything. Except the future. We hadn't talked of that.

One afternoon, when he'd sat holding my hand and saying nothing for a long time, I turned and studied his face, brooding and strong in the reflected firelight.

"The buccaneer in the laboratory," I said.

"Hum?"

"You look like a pirate to me, Michael. Or a cavalier. I wouldn't be surprised to find you kept a falcon in your room and went hawking in your spare time."

He smiled. "I haven't any spare time. Anyway, this isn't the age of falcons. It's the age of—"

"Of what?" I prompted.

"Parakeets?" he said with a grin.

I threw my arms about him, laughing. "Not for us," I said, my lips against his ear. "We'll be adventurers." Then, when the implication of what I'd said reached me —the assumption of a shared future, which he had never

7

spoken of—I drew away from him, flushing.

Michael held onto my hand and looked at me for a long moment and said, "You are a very romantic girl, with a head full of story books. All right, then, adventurers. Aren't you going to hold out for your lines?"

"Don't tease," I said, quite unable to tell if the sensation I felt was pleasure or pain. Was he proposing to me? Propositioning me? He had never said he loved me. I knew, the way you do know when you're loved, but I did not know what he wanted of me. My life shared with his, or a pretty—perhaps passionate—memory to paste in his scrapbook before the doors of the laboratory closed on him again for years?

"Was I teasing?" he said. "Forgive me." And then he added, "I love you, Ella."

Joy is a strange thing. What I mean is, people accept joy in strange ways, because of what they are, what they've expected, how they feel about themselves. Michael's words brought me the first great joy of my life, and yet I was never so aware of my plainness as I was then. How had I won him, how would I hold him? Happiness entered that room like a presence, and I didn't dare take it completely, or look at it directly. It was as if it would disappear if I turned my face full upon it, acceptingly. I think Michael might have proposed to me that day if I hadn't fluttered away from this flame of joy like a moth barely making it back to the shadows.

I went to my room that night saying to myself, He loves me. Michael is in love with me. Over and over the knowledge lifted me like a deep, shining wave, and over and over I crashed, wondering, Why? For how long? I finally fell asleep in despair, realizing that, for all I had laughed and sold myself on that charm, I didn't really believe in it. It seemed that I was one of those people too insecure to accept happiness, to believe in love. I only hadn't known it until love and real happiness came along.

In the morning my father, not usually an observant man, said, "What's wrong with you, Ella? Are you sick?"

"In a way," I answered listlessly. Then, because this one love I knew without a doubt, I said, "I'm sick because Michael told me he loved me, and I can't believe him."

"Can't believe him? I'd believe anything he said. I should say he was incapable of pretending."

"Yes. I know that. With my mind. My mind isn't getting a look-in. All the rest of me keeps remembering that . . . that I'm not beautiful," I said flatly. "I'm not even pretty."

Dad frowned and turned his head from side to side, sadly. "I never would have thought your standards to be so shallow, Ella. I would never have thought it. Love doesn't parade around like Miss America in a bathing suit."

He doesn't, I said to myself, deny my words. He doesn't tell me I *am* pretty. He worries about my values, but I want to have spun-gold hair.

"Oh, I know," I said. "I sound as if appearances were all that mattered, and of course I know it isn't so. It's just . . . it's just—" But I didn't know what it was just.

"Beauty," said my father, who is devoted to the homely homily, "is in the beholder's eye."

"Yes, Dad," I said humbly. But I don't like homilies. They unnerve me, since it's obvious that their purpose is to gloss an inadequacy. People don't need to be told that it's all for the best unless something awful has happened, or that someday they'll laugh at all this, if at the moment they can do anything but cry. Being told that beauty is in the beholder's eye is being told that you're plain but somebody loves you anyway. I just couldn't stand it.

My feelings were shallow and I knew it, but also bitterly sincere and utterly confused. I'd look at myself in a mirror and think, You, hold Michael? It's impossible. I'd look away and think, Do you suppose Michael's standards are as superficial as your own? You don't deserve him.

All the time that Michael had to give, away from his work, he gave to me. He even contrived to give me more than formerly, at the cost, I guess, of sleep. And he seemed so tranquilly happy, so secure, so without misgiving.

My father had misgivings. He said to me rather sharply one day, "Are you still wasting your time and happiness worrying over your looks?"

"No." I didn't expect him to believe me, and he didn't.

"Ella," he said, "let me say this, and then let's put the whole nonesense behind us, please. You have looks that are exceedingly appealing to a certain type of man. Michael's type. I might add, my type. You look like your mother."

I wanted to say something, but couldn't, and after a moment he went on.

"Your mother was lovely. Her looks were informed by her spirit and her mind. They were not just a matter of features. It's the same with you. You have—you *had*, until all this farrago came up—an excellent mind. I cannot tell you how it grieves me to see it rambling this way after some peculiar stereotype of beauty that wouldn't become you if you suddenly had it. I don't know why Michael hasn't noticed the way you're behaving—"

"Because he's like you, Dad. Not awfully observant of people."

"Doesn't look for trouble, you mean. And he feels secure with you. Well, he'll notice, sooner or later, and then I'll tell you what he'll think. The truth simply won't occur to him, because looks don't matter to Michael," said my father, who'd just finished telling me I was appealing. "He'll think you don't really care for him."

"Oh, no," I said, seriously alarmed.

"I'm afraid yes."

What he said, I feared, might be true. What he didn't understand is that a woman wants to be everything for the man she loves. And beauty is part of everything.

Still, I tried to put the whole problem (which I had made a problem) away from me. Michael, in his twenty-four years, had not been immured from beautiful girls, and he had fallen in love with me. I told myself that that should be answer enough, and it very nearly was.

The Beautiful Friend

Each year, shortly after January first, Dad gives an Open House for faculty, wives, graduate students and other acquaintances. Martha, who is cook, maid, and general everything, helps me with it, and we keep it simple. Eggnog and fruitcake. Even that is madly occupying, since there are usually about one hundred and fifty guests. We like it.

On the morning of the Eggnog, as we call it, Martha and I were up early in the kitchen, checking the fruitcakes (we make them ourselves, in October), the brandy, the punch bowls and glasses. I had asked the florist to deliver the flowers as soon as possible after he opened, and I thought it was he when the doorbell rang.

"At the front," Martha muttered. She was looking in the refrigerator, deciding whether we had enough cream. "Tell him to bring them round the back. That hall rug is vacuumed for the day."

The bell rang again and I hurried to the front door and opened it not to the florist but to Michael.

"Why, Michael," I said, feeling that rush of pleasure and pride and sheer delight that the sight of him, expected or unexpected, always gives me. "This is an odd hour to call."

"Even odder, when you hear what for," he said, coming into the hall. He put his arms around me and I felt the fresh coldness of his cheek against mine, and then his lips, cool and tender, on mine. The January morning poured in the open door and I heard the oil burner start up as if violently awakened. But Michael just held me, not speaking, as he would have after a long absence.

"Darling," I said at last, very gently for fear of disturbing his mood, "it's winter, and it's coming in the house."

He put one arm back and shoved the door shut. "It's spring," he said. "It's the beginning of everything. Will you marry me?"

I closed my eyes and leaned against him and wondered if he would ever know how much I loved him, and wondered if that really mattered. Just so we did, just so we would be together. "Oh, Michael, yes," I said.

We went into the library and sat on the sofa, our hands clasped. I couldn't speak, but Michael, looking buoyant and happy, wanted to talk.

"I decided last night that we're just wasting time apart that ought to be time together," he said. "If you want to wait until you graduate, that's all right, but it suddenly occurred to me that I'd better let you know where I stood. In case you didn't know. And find out, you know, where you stand." For Michael, he was touchingly inarticulate.

"But you knew," I said. "There wasn't any question."

"I thought we'd better get it into words. And once I decided, it just seemed too long to wait until tomorrow."

"Aren't you coming to the Eggnog?"

"I didn't want to propose to you at a party."

"But you are coming?"

He grinned and nodded. "For you, anything." To Michael, more than four people gathered together is a crush, but he'd agreed to come to the Eggnog. In the olden days he'd have slain dragons for his love. These days he braved parties.

"I think you're wonderful," I said, and he smiled and didn't deny it.

Martha came in presently to see why I'd deserted, and at the same time Dad returned from his morning walk. We told them, and there was so much happiness, so many words, so many plans and decisions and revisions that it's a wonder the Eggnog ever got assembled, but it did. Dad went off to his study, saying he wouldn't encumber us with his help, and after a while Michael left, giving me a long, sweet, parting kiss. I wandered, cloaked with joy, through the preparations, and Martha smiled and smiled.

It was lovely, lovely. . . .

In the late afternoon the phone rang as I was going through the hall. I picked it up and heard Mady's glad, confident voice.

"I'm in town with my parents, we're at the Statler, I can't *wait* to see you. What are you doing this minute?"

For the first time since I'd known her, my heart dipped a little at the thought of seeing Mady. I wouldn't admit to myself why. I wouldn't even admit it was so, but part of me knew it and wondered hastily, disloyally, whether I could get out of having her here. I did not give this unworthy impulse a hearing.

"What I'm doing this minute," I said brightly and warmly and not insincerely—this, after all, was Mady, my friend—"is being delighted that you're here. It's Dad's Open House day. Do you think your parents would come, too?"

"Adore it, I'm sure. Listen, lamb, I can spend the night

and we'll have a long old talk about everything."

"That's wonderful," I said, "I can hardly wait."

We hung up, and I looked in the mirror over the console table for a moment and then told Martha I was going to get dressed. I didn't. Not immediately. I sat in the big window seat in my bedroom and looked at the bony trees and the patches of dark ice on the street and thought that the time had come for a moment of what is called seaching self-encounter. Now. Later wouldn't do.

How did I feel about Mady's coming?

To have her in a room with Michael and expect her not to flirt with him would be like counting on a flower not to bloom in the sun. And when Mady flirted . . .

But if she knew we were engaged? Mady was no poacher, but actually that might be even worse. She'd be so delicious about me (quite without malice) that she might be irresistible. I'd known it to happen. *Why* did she have to call today? I thought moodily. Only, of course, which day, or even which beautiful girl, didn't matter.

What it came to was that I could spend the rest of my life—my life with Michael—running scared of all beautiful women, and so run an excellent chance of ruining that life, or I could believe what I had every reason to believe, that Michael loved and wanted me as I was.

There, I said to myself, as if I'd settled something, and went to run a tub.

Mady and her parents came when the party was at its peak. Naturally. She looked ravishing. Anyone beholding with even half an eye would see that. And, to my joy and relief, I found I was glad to see her. All I could remember was that we were friends, and I began to have a little hope for my character after all.

When the first greetings were over, and her parents had gone off with my father to mingle, Mady began to look around with bright interest. Her eyes sought something to divert and hold her, the way Mady's eyes always do. They sped over the older faculty members, over the women, lingered here and there on instructors, stopped with complete finality on Michael, across the room.

"Oh, my," she said in a tone of delectation, "take me to that leader, please." Her self-confidence was, as always, quite stunning.

I hesitated, and then said, "It's Michael. He . . . we're going to be married."

She turned large astonished eyes on me. "Lambie," she breathed. "How in the world did you do it? *I* haven't been within shooting distance of anything like that." She didn't mean to be sarcastic or ungracious. She simply, honestly, couldn't understand how I had won someone like Michael when she had not. Neither could I.

"I did it by being my own sweet self," I said, and I guess I *was* a bit sarcastic. Mady didn't pay any attention. She patted my hand, shook her head, sighed and said, "Well . . . I'll certainly have to meet him."

Michael, who had spied us, was making his way across the room. I introduced them and felt like saying, "Be careful, there aren't any copies," and then Martha beckoned to me and I had to leave.

It seemed ages before I could look for them again, and then they weren't in the living room. I went out into the hall, where a few people were leaving, and said goodbye to them, and got away and went toward the library, which Michael always made for. They were there. Sitting on the sofa, their backs to me, their voices soft and audible.

"I was very lonely when I met Ella," Michael was saying.

And Mady, in her clear caressing tones, "Of course. I understand perfectly. With you so lonesome and her so winsome . . . She's really an adorable girl—"

I said to myself, This isn't the way it sounds. I can just walk in here and be welcome and not be interrupting anything. It is not what it sounds.

But I backed away like a sneak thief and went to the living room and mingled and mingled, seeing to it that Dad's Eggnog was a success. I kept telling myself that any minute they'd be back, that it didn't matter if they weren't, that what I'd heard was out of context. And I kept feeling worse and worse. I kept feeling, in some peculiar way, vindicated, as if the unworthy part of me had known better than the worthy part.

When Dad and I had seen the last guest from the door (except Mady's parents, who were staying for dinner and had gone upstairs to rest) Michael and Mady wandered into the hall.

"Everybody gone?" Michael asked, trying to sound chagrined.

My father laughed. "As if you didn't know. Michael,

when you get older you won't hate parties so much. I remember I used to. Funny thing—I sort of enjoy them now." He looked at Mady with that pleased expression men get at the sight of her. "But you, now, Mady. Never known you to miss a party before."

She never met Michael before, I thought miserably.

Mady smiled around at us. "I thought it was more important to know Michael," she said. Mady is always forthright. She linked her arm through my father's and led him toward the library. "And now I'm going to pump you."

My face felt starched, my knees weak, and I didn't look at Michael at all. Let him go after her, I thought. Then I'll go upstairs and collapse with my justified suspicions.

He said, "Let's take a walk. You look wan from all the smoke and people."

I wanted to say, It isn't from smoke and people. I wanted to say, I don't want to take a walk, I want to go to my room and get on with my crying. . . .

I let him get his jacket and my fleecy coat and I went with him into the frigid dusk and we walked alone, unspeaking, for two cold blocks.

"I had a nice talk with your friend," he said casually.

"I know. About how lonely you were when you met me." I hadn't meant to say it, but it was said. Michael looked at me in surprise. "I wasn't eavesdropping," I said defensively. "I was looking for you."

"Then why didn't you come in when you found us?"

Us, I thought, twisting the word in my mind. "Martha called me."

"Oh." He took my hand and we walked, and I realized that we might be back at the house before he said another word. Michael's like that. This time I couldn't stand it. "Why were you telling her that?" I said.

"Telling who what?"

"Mady. That you were so lonesome before you met me," I said evenly.

"Because it's true. Until I met you, I didn't really have any person who gave my life purpose. I had work, of course, but I've always known work wasn't enough. And then, when I met you—" he smiled at me "—I knew what I'd been waiting for, that's all."

My real moment of self-encounter was there. A self loved for herself. The certainty that without beauty I was nothing fell away in the frozen air. I didn't even bother to be ashamed of what I'd been thinking. I just gave in and was happy.

I said, as a confident and happy girl will, "I'm so glad you liked Mady. I'm very fond of her."

"She is of you."

"I know. In school," I went on tentatively, "we were known as the plain girl and the beautiful friend." Never let well enough alone, I thought, furious with myself. Still, assurance isn't mastered in a moment—

I became aware that Michael was looking at me with considerable vexation. "Ella," he said. "Nobody in his right mind would call that girl plain, and I don't think it's becoming of you to talk that way. People who didn't know you would think you were vain."

I thought he was teasing. Heartlessly. And then I saw

that Michael, who can never pretend, was perfectly serious. I didn't understand it then, and I don't understand it now, but in this beholder's eye I was the beautiful one. And there for one long moment I was, even to myself. It felt fine, but I was willing to let it go. I was not willing to have Michael think me vain.

"Darling," I said. "It was the other way around."

Michael laughed and hugged me and said, "All right. I guess you have a right to be vain now and then. You love me in spite of my preoccupation and I'll love you in spite of your conceit. Settled?"

There it was. I couldn't get him to believe I wasn't beautiful, and it was the last time I tried.

The Turning Point

*J*ane Martin, looking at the back of the *Herald,* considered her father, who faced the front of it. She contemplated and discarded two or three opening sentences which might cause him to drop the upper half of the newspaper and pay attention to her. She glanced at her mother, who lifted inquiring brows, but Jane, whose problem lay behind the *Herald,* merely smiled and shifted her eyes to the paper wall.

Someone had robbed a hotel, she read, and made off with a lot of jewelry. Someone had punched a bus driver. A kangaroo had had a baby. All the trivia at the back. Her father dealt with vital matters in the front.

"Dad?"

The merest rustle of paper to indicate he'd heard.

"I have an eight-thirty class, and I have to tell you something before I go. Daddy?"

As she'd expected, the Daddy attracted him. It was what he liked her to call him.

He allowed the top half of the paper to fold over,

studied his daughter pleasantly. His glance approved her violet tweed suit, her white blouse, her shining brown hair and eyes.

"What is it, honey?"

Jane hesitated, then said rapidly, "I have a date tonight." She paid no attention to his suddenly bland expression. "It's someone . . . somebody new. He's coming for me here at seven-thirty." She stopped, a bit breathless.

"And so?" her father inquired.

Jane looked to her mother once again, to meet an understanding nod. She rubbed one hand along her arm. "So this, Dad," she said gently, very clearly. "I want you to hear his name. Now. It's Richard Carpenter. Richard. His name *is not George.*"

Mr. Martin looked mildly amazed. "And why should his name be George, rather than . . . than whatever it is?"

"Richard," his daughter repeated. "His name is Richard Carpenter."

"Yes. Than Richard, as you say."

"There's no reason why it should be George. I never have known anyone named George, as a matter of fact," Jane said in a loud tone.

"Is this apology, or regret?" her father twinkled. He showed signs of returning to the *Herald.*

Jane stood up, leaving her coffee untouched, and most of her toast and egg. "It's explanation, that's all. I'm simply trying to tell you that the boy who is coming tonight will be named Richard, and I sort of wish you wouldn't call him George."

"No reason why I should, is there?"

Mrs. Martin entered the conversation. "I think it's ridiculous," she said, and added "dear," to soften her attack, "for you to pretend you don't know what Jane is talking about. You call them all George, and you know you do."

Mr. Martin looked astounded, and Jane said irritably, "I don't know what you mean by *all*. There hasn't been *any* for ages. And I don't blame them. How would you like to call for a date and then get treated like a leak in the roof?"

"That's an odd metaphor," Mr. Martin said with interest. "Or is it a simile?"

Jane turned away. "I have to leave. I'm late now."

"Jane," her father called after her, "don't be huffy. I'll remember that . . . that what's-his-name . . . isn't George. What *is* it, again?"

Jane slammed the front door behind her, and they saw her pass the window, walking with hard little heel clicks, toward the bus stop.

Mr. Martin rubbed his mustache and looked warily at his wife. "Now, what was that all about?"

His wife started to clear the table. "I think you know. You've driven away most of the boys she's met since she started college, and the ones before that, too, with . . . with your . . ."

She broke off, helpless to explain or avert what her husband did to the young men who came to call on Jane. Young men who came once or twice and disappeared. She dropped a fork, retrieved it, and continued, "It's insulting to be called George if—"

"Don't see why," her husband interrupted jovially. "I had an uncle, name of George. Never seemed to chafe him any."

Mrs. Martin studied him coldly. "That's not amusing. Of course boys mind a girl's father not being interested— not even being polite enough—to remember *what* their names are. The trouble with you," she said, "is that you won't admit Jane is grown-up."

"Let's say growing-up, shall we? She's only eighteen."

Mrs. Martin, who wanted to slam a door herself, said sadly, "You may be very sorry someday, for what you're doing now." She turned toward the kitchen.

He shrugged a little and called after her, "So far as I'm concerned, they can't really be interested or they wouldn't let any old father or what he called them get in the way."

At the sink, Mrs. Martin heard his protest and the note of half-apology it contained. But she didn't answer. Instead, she stood at the window, looking out at the autumn garden, wondering why the mother-in-law was so ill-sung. A girl's father could be a greater menace, if his will was strong, than any mere mother or mother-in-law. She thought it would come as no surprise to find a father behind many a spinster fading out of loveliness, alone and not sure how it had happened.

"Besides—" Her husband carried his dishes into the kitchen as a gesture of truce. "Besides, I don't like the people she dates. When I *like* one, then I'll be very reasonable." His tone indicated that he was being quite reasonable now.

His wife did not reply.

Jane ran down the street under the gold and scarlet trees, missed the bus that would have got her to the university in time for the eight-thirty French class, and leaned, a little breathless, against a lamp post.

If I'd had any foresight, she told herself, I'd have gone away to school. Just because she lived in a college town, did it mean she had to go to school there? But, of course, it did. Financially, it was almost necessary. And then, last year when she'd made her choice, she hadn't really wanted to leave home. If you were an only child, and if you loved your parents, you didn't simply go off to school because you thought it would be more exciting. If now and then you felt defrauded of the specialness of college (which to you wasn't much different from high school—just in another part of town) you were still able to recognize that as a not vital complaint.

She stepped away from the lamp post, burrowing for a coin, as the bus charged toward her. Still, she thought, grabbing for a strap and shifting her books, still it did sometimes seem that for a girl whose looks had never frightened anyone, whose conversation and disposition were passable, she had a noticeably empty space in her life that should have been filled and labeled *Dates*. Or maybe *Men*.

Last year she still hadn't minded much that dates were

not a part of her life, the way they were with most girls she knew. She'd felt sort of special, different. She remembered even saying to people, "Oh, I'd rather go to a show with Daddy. It's fun."

And, suddenly, it was not fun. It was something oppressive, that insisted she was a child, that overlooked her rights as a person.

This morning at breakfast she had made a slight stand for these rights. Oh, not much of a one. Enough to put a question, slam a door. She was rather sorry about the door—you shouldn't be rude to your father. But your father shouldn't be rude to your friends. Thinking this, she sighed nervously and wondered if dates were really worth the trouble they caused at home. I've never really had fun on one, she thought. Not one with a boy.

Passing the library building, she looked at her watch, decided to skip the French class altogether. Today, she said to herself, I shall not produce my awkward version of what I think Verlaine had in mind when he wrote *Fêtes galantes.* He had love and romance in mind, and put it very beautifully in French. How should I put it into English? What is there about romance that I know well enough to translate from one language to another?

She went into the library, through the stacks to the History section. History, now—that was capable of being grasped by any mind earnest enough to try. You needn't be a singer of serenades to comprehend the import of Disraeli brooding over the Suez Canal.

Richard Carpenter presented himself at the Martins' at precisely seven-thirty. He was a science major, and apt to be meticulous about such things. In an unassuming way he was quite attractive, Jane thought. A nice sort of height and weight. Quick, intelligent eyes. She'd had Cokes with him between classes several times this term, but tonight was their first proper date. The first one involving a set hour, the meeting of parents in a tidied living room, the suggestion of a movie if there was any she'd like particularly to see.

It was all very normal, was being enacted in thousands of homes at just this moment, was nothing at all to worry about.

But Jane, meeting him at the door, leading him to the tidied living room, was worried.

"Mom, Dad," she said in an over-pleasant voice, "this is Richard. Richard Carpenter."

She pulled her date forward so that his bulk would catch the eye of her father, who seemed unaware, as yet, that anyone had entered the room at all. A little courtesy, Jane was thinking. Just a little, please . . .

"Hello, Richard," Mrs. Martin said, coming forward with outstretched hand and a smile. "How nice to have you here." She looked quickly at her husband. "Here's Richard, dear, come to take Jane out."

Mr. Martin looked up with an air of surprise. "Oh?" He got to his feet. His voice grew faintly puzzled, very faintly hurt. He didn't look at Richard, but at Jane. "Are you going out tonight, honey?" He mused, then smiled.

"It's all right. What Dad had in mind will wait. It doesn't really matter. . . ." His voice trailed away, and abruptly he became aware of Richard. "Youth calls to youth, doesn't it, Mr. . . . ah . . . Anyway, that's what they always say, eh?" He put out his hand, smiling.

" 'Spect so," Richard said uneasily.

Knowing she shouldn't, knowing she didn't even want to, Jane put to her alertly waiting father the question she knew he wanted. "Was there something special you had in mind, Dad? You know, I told you this morning that Richard and I were going out—"

"Yes, yes, of course. I'm afraid I forgot." His glance moved over Richard, who seemed all at once ungainly, rather gauche.

The boy looked from Jane to her father, then said cheerfully, "Well, sir, I sure wouldn't want to—" He stopped. "We did sort of plan to take in a show. Or something."

Mr. Martin brightened. "Oh, well, then, if you haven't anything really definite in mind—" His wife stepped forward, a little flare of anger in her eyes, but he continued smoothly, "How about all of us listening together?"

"Listening to what?" Jane asked flatly, as Richard hesitated.

"Why, to my new Brahms quartet. I got it especially for you, honey," he said appealingly to Jane. "It's the London recording you wanted so much." He strode briskly to the phonograph. "This is just great, kids. Just great. We'll have the Brahms, then perhaps a little Haydn for a chaser, eh? And then—" He looked around, laughing, snapping his fingers as an idea appeared to strike him. "And then I'll take the whole bunch of us out for a soda or something. How's that?" He posed by the phonograph, face alight, waiting for their response.

They dropped Richard at his fraternity-house door at about eleven o'clock, and drove home in silence, the three of them together in the front seat. Jane said good night to her parents and went upstairs while Mr. Martin put the car away.

She undressed slowly, washed in an absent-minded way, then got into bed and lay staring at the ceiling.

Is this how it's going to be? she thought. Always? Mother can't help me. I never seem to help myself. I'm eighteen years old, but I don't even know how to have a date. Only, until tonight I at least always got them out of the house. Am I to have my dates at home from now on?

Downstairs, she heard her mother trying to help her.

"This has been perfectly disgraceful," her mother was saying.

It certainly has, said Jane to herself.

"What's been disgraceful?" Mr. Martin demanded. "Don't be fanciful, dear. We all had a fine evening."

Nobody had a fine evening, not even you, Daddy dear.

"Who had a fine evening?" her mother asked. "Did you?"

"Will somebody tell me what all the fuss is about?"

What's the fuss ever about, Daddy, if not about you?

"What's the boy's name?" her mother said. "Do you remember?"

"Naturally, I remember. I've been told it often enough. It's Richard. Richard Carpenter."

"Well—" her mother's voice grew loud—"Well, then, why did you call him George?"

Yes, why? We said good night to him, and you'd never called him anything but "you" all evening, so why did you say, "Good night, George," as he went up his porch steps?

"Did I?" her father asked in his very surprised tone. "Force of habit, I guess. She's known so many boys named George."

Jane put her head in the pillow and bit hard as the tears came.

One day a week or so later, Jane was walking across the campus alone, scuffing through autumn-strewn leaves and breathing the special air of October, a combination of leaf smoke, apples and well-sunned breezes, when, without conscious intention, she sat down on a bench to reorganize her life.

She lit a cigarette, leaned back and said to herself, I'm going to make some sort of decision now. I'm going to reach a conclusion and then act upon it. Assuming my father will not change his attitude, and I can't assume anything else, what am I going to do about it?

She puffed at her cigarette thoughtfully. It was a recent gesture, this smoking of hers. Defiance of a sort. Against what? Against whom? Well, that's clear enough, she said to herself. I'm trying to demonstrate to my father the fact of my maturity. In this little, sort of silly way I'm announcing to him that I've come of age.

But this morning he had casually offered her a light, making no comment at all. Her mother had said, "Smoking, dear?" in a mild reproving tone, and Mr. Martin had inquired, "Why shouldn't she?" inferentially on his daughter's side against silly parental taboos.

Jane stubbed out the cigarette that had proved no wedge between her and her father. She dropped it into a trash can behind the bench.

There, she thought, leaning back. There. That's what I've been thinking, and that's what I've been wanting. A wedge between me and Dad. Possibly even a large space. It shouldn't have to be this way, if he would understand that I'm not still a little girl thinking Daddy the only man in the world. But he doesn't understand it, and never will.

It didn't have to be this way, yet this was the way it was. Love, loyalty, on one side. On the other, a sense of injustice being done to her as a person. And, with it all, a feeling of loss. Something that had once been warmth and protection and laughter had become a suffocating box, a cage with a hood over it.

I will not be closed up this way, she thought with nervous defiance. I just will not.

"Hi, Jane."

Here was Richard Carpenter, whom she hadn't seen since the night of their musicale. He hovered uncertainly beside the bench. She thought it nice of him to have stopped at all. Perhaps he'd been afraid she'd seen him. Richard wouldn't be rude. But she wondered why he didn't go on after they'd exchanged a few words. Surely he didn't crave another double date with her parents?

"Mind if I sit down?" he asked.

Jane shook her head. "Of course I don't. I'd like it," she added truthfully.

He studied her a moment. "I've been awfully busy."

Jane smiled.

"No, really. I had a term paper that was overdue. I've been . . . meaning to phone you."

"That's nice," she said when the silence had gone on too long.

"Yeah," he answered absently. He leaned forward a little. "Look, Jane. There's a coffee dance at our House, Sunday afternoon. Suppose you could go with me?"

"I'd love to," she said softly.

"Well, how about it?"

They looked at each other wordlessly, the problem apparent, if unspoken. Then Jane, who knew about the etiquette of well-bred girls, suggested something unacceptable to it but, it seemed, necessary to her happiness now. "I could meet you somewhere."

Richard looked uncomfortable. "It . . . that might be better. It's . . . uh . . . I hate to have you— But yes, I guess that'd be best. The dance'll only last two hours, and we'd hate to be . . . we wouldn't want to be held up."

He means he'd like to get to it at all, Jane thought. "All right, Richard. Where shall I . . . I mean, how?"

They planned a meeting down the street, Jane to say she was going to a sorority house, Richard to pick her up around the corner from her house. Their voices were strained, their eyes, when they met each other's, restless.

Still, Jane thought gratefully, he must like me, to bother at all.

On Sunday afternoon she put on her black taffeta afternoon dress with its full skirt. She clasped a choker of small pearls at her neck and fastened her hair in an intricate French roll. Her face was immobile. She felt neither daring nor ashamed, neither anxious nor reluctant about the dance.

She liked Richard, but it was certainly not for love of him that she was about to sneak out of her house on a lie. She loved her father, but affection for him did not include sharing every bit of her life with him. She did not like secrets, but knew they began here, this afternoon, for her.

Downstairs, as she stopped in the doorway, her father said, "Aren't you pretty? A bit dressed up, surely, for an afternoon at a girls' sorority?"

"These girls dress more for each other than for boys, I think," her mother said. "Isn't that right, Jane?"

"I guess so," Jane answered calmly. "It's a tea, Daddy. A lot of girls having tea together."

Deliberately she enlarged upon her untruths, and she knew this sort of self-punishment was going to make the dance less fun, though she certainly intended to have fun at it. She was punishing her father, too, though he'd have to remain unaware of it.

She thought, going around the corner to meet Richard, that from now on her father would be unaware of a lot that he might have shared. If he'd known how to share.

At home, Mr. Martin got up and went to his record cabinet. Selecting a Debussy nocturne, he put it on the turntable and said to his wife as the violins began to sing, "I like to see her having fun with other girls." There was approval in his tone. "After all, she's only eighteen."

"Yes," said Mrs. Martin. "She's eighteen." And you just lost her for good, she added silently, studying her husband's face for some awareness, some regret. There was none.

He smiled at her peacefully and said, "I didn't like that last fellow, anyway . . . whatever-his-name-was." Closing his eyes, he listened to the music.

The Sari

I never make the train, the plane, the bus, the boat with anything like a minute to spare, and the Denver-New York flight that day last September was no exception. It was all but in the air when I dashed up the steps, virtually into the arms of the frowning hostess. No airline hostess has ever smiled at me in greeting.

"You almost missed the flight," she said reprovingly.

"But *made* it," I said, supplying the smile.

She waved me down the aisle and I dropped into the only vacant space, fastened the seat buckle and tried to catch my breath.

"You certainly haven't changed much," said the person at the window seat (I never get a window seat) and I turned to find Annabel Browning beside me. I don't dote on Annabel, but she was better than the salesman I usually sit next to—the one who starts out talking about his family and ends up talking about a little dinner for two when the plane lands. Annabel and I had been roommates (assigned) our first year in college, and had separated, by mutual agreement, at the end of the winter term. I'm told she found me and my attitudes unbearably haphazard. I state as a fact that I found her the most immature person I knew. I mean, by the time you're in college, you should have a glimmering of the fact that you are appended to the world, and not vice versa.

Still, all that was in the pretty distant past, and I was grateful to her for not being that salesman, so I said brightly, "Annabel . . . what a nice surprise," and was glad I'd worn my Chanely suit and had just had my hair done. Annabel doesn't look at people, she inspects them.

After a moment she said, "You're looking quite well, Frances," as if it were an admission.

"So are you."

She was, of course, looking gorgeous, but there was no need for me to tell her this. Her mirror, her mother and every man who'd looked at her that morning had undoubtedly already done so.

"How are your parents?" she asked.

"They're fine. How're yours?"

"Oh, they're fine. Did you have a good summer?"

"Dandy," I said, and sighed. Even a jet flight was going to be overlong if we couldn't make some improvement here. We both live in Denver and go to the same girls' college in New England. All similarity or concord between us ended there.

With most people, one wouldn't assume that the entire trip was to be spent in conversation, however inane. Actually, I had a quite good novel with me, and would have been happy to get on with it. Or pretend to get on with it while I occupied myself with my thoughts, equally happy. But with Annabel this was impossible unless one were willing to appear unfriendly, and I was not. I felt too marvelous.

It had been a wonderful vacation, and I was looking forward now to my senior year and graduation. I'd been going to school just about long enough, and could scarcely wait to get out into what commencement speakers still refer to as The World—implying that school is something else again, and perhaps they're right, at that.

Over and above and, I confess, slightly to one side of all this was the consciousness of that class ring hanging on a thin gold chain around my neck. I hadn't precisely decided to *marry* the donor, who hadn't, either, precisely asked me, but I did find him the most exciting and somehow, at the same time, the most endearing man I'd known. I was looking forward to a year of his handsome attendance. When the year was over? Well, who knew? He, too, would be part of the World I'd be going into.

"Aren't you glad this is the last year?" I said to Annabel's perfect profile.

"Why?" she said, not turning.

"Oh—" I waved my hands. "It's all too big to go into words. The World, Annabel, the World. I want to get out in it."

"Why?" she said again.

I decided to be unfriendly after all, and opened my novel so I could think without interruption. I hadn't found my place before Annabel said, "I'm sorry if I was abrupt. It's just that I've been thinking what a miserable

37

summer it's been. For me, I mean."

I sighed again, suppressing it decently, I hope. Annabel is, always has been, no doubt will continue to be, a confider. She doesn't care whom she confides in, just so whoever it is listens, and she assumes, with that spring-green ego of hers, that we are all breathlessly concerned with her affairs.

I've always found her startlingly candid, far franker about herself than most of us can afford to be. But, then, it probably comes from her great self-confidence. People who have it to the extent Annabel does even take pleasure in detailing their errors and shortcomings. Charmingly, of course. The thing is to make your confession of failure sound like a triumph, and it can be done. By the Annabels.

Well, I thought, closing my book, it can't hurt to listen. There'd been a time when I used to get furious with her, and compare myself to The Wedding Guest. But I was older now, and kinder . . . less willing to label a matter trivia simply because it didn't interest me.

"What happened?" I asked.

She continued to stare straight ahead, like someone reciting, and said, "I broke my engagement."

"Oh? I didn't know you were. Engaged, that is."

She hesitated. "Well, maybe not formally, but I had his class ring." Her lip quivered, and she tilted her chin in the air.

"You've probably given back a baker's dozen of them, haven't you?" I said cheerfully. It was meant to be a compliment, but Annabel didn't take it that way. Her lids descended and I sensed a pained silence. At the same time I remembered that she was active in the school drama society. Small of me.

"Who was it?" I asked, to make up.

"His name is Whit Larsen."

I gave a start that almost propelled me into the seat in front, but unobservant Annabel duly failed to observe how well she'd caught my attention. She went on looking like Nefertiti, while I tried to assemble my dispersed wits.

Whit Larsen and Annabel? There was some awful mistake. It was Whit and I. Whit and Frances. It had been for over a month, in actuality, and last night Whit had told me it had been so from the beginning of time. Words that can only sound trite to someone not in love.

I'd only met him at the beginning of the summer. He, too, lived in Denver and went to school in the East. I'd had a vacation job as a stenographer in his father's importing firm, and had admired him, from a distance, starting my first day there. About a month ago he'd reduced the distance to nothing and we'd been together steadily ever since.

I couldn't honestly say I knew what love was, but I knew I felt something for Whit Larsen that I'd never felt for anyone else. He'd given me his ring the night before, and it was *Whit and Frances*. Nothing, no one else.

He had never mentioned Annabel Browning. Without saying so, he'd let me feel that no one had had that ring before. Oh, I knew he was an almost compulsive flirt, but

I put that down to his extraordinary looks and the way in which women turned almost carnivorous at the sight of him. It would have taken a stronger man than Whit to resist, and who was I to demand such strength from anybody? When I become flawless, I'd tell myself, then I'll start criticizing Whit. And though I'd feel my cheeks grow warm when he'd turn from me to watch a pretty girl go by, I'd remember that it was I, and not some other girl, that he spent his time with. What's in a glance? I'd say to my pride. He doesn't mean anything by it. And then he'd turn back to me, with that smile, and put his hand over mine, and I'd be at peace.

So now, in the plane, I began again to rationalize his behavior. He hadn't told me about Annabel because he'd thought I'd be hurt. He was, after all, twenty-one years old. Small wonder that another girl had worn this very ring before me, and no cause for bitterness or repine. Yet in my imagination the ring that had lain light and warm against my heart suddenly felt a little heavy, a trifle cold.

Feeling mendacious, I said to Annabel, "When did you . . . break the engagement? I mean, give him back his ring?"

"About a month ago," she said broodingly.

And no one's replaced him? I thought. Annabel was not known for her steadfastness. Had she cared for him so much, then? A month. How many days had he allowed to elapse between getting the ring back from her and seeing someone else it might be fun to give it to? This was not so easy to rationalize as those long glances away from me had been. I began to wonder if he'd ever worn the ring himself at all. Maybe it had just gone from girl to girl, like the potato in a relay race, I thought bitterly.

Now completely committed to hypocrisy, I said to Annabel, "Would it make you feel better to talk about it?"

It would, and she did.

She'd gone last year to Winter Carnival with someone who was neither here nor there, but simply a chance to get to Winter Carnival. On the night of the big dance, clasped in this nondescript's arms, she'd seen, over his shoulder, Whit Larsen lounging against the wall, eyes traveling the room imperiously. Composed, handsome, arms crossed and brows lifted, he'd looked like a young laird surveying the ball, deciding just which maiden to carry off in his coach and four.

Annabel, who'd merely been going through the motions of enjoyment, suddenly alerted. She could feel her eyes begin to shine, her skin and hair to glow, her smile to flash, and the nondescript looked at her with delight.

"Man, that's more real," he said. "Like I thought you were bored, or something."

"Bored?" She laughed and tossed her gleaming head. "Bored, my pet? What in the world makes you think that —uh—" *Whatever-your-name-is,* she said to herself, and that amused her so that her eyes simply danced, looking up to his.

"Well," he said, warming, "like you haven't uttered word one in an hour."

"But I've been *dancing*. Silly boy," she added, to see how he'd take it. He took it as she'd expected, with fatuous pleasure, and by now her enjoyment was so complete that she all but forgot what had set it in motion.

Then Whit cut in.

The nondescript frowned and said, "Hey. Quelle gives?"

"Rules of the road, my boy," said Whit. "Vehicles on the right have precedence. I'm on your right."

"Well, I'll be back, road-toad," said the nondescript as he backed off, and Annabel leaned against Whit with pure pleasure, dancing away in his arms.

"That's the way he's been talking ever since I got here," she said with her molten giggle. "Like he's a luke-warm cat, you know? A larder full of last year's prep-school twaddle."

"How did that cat get a kitten like you, is what I'd like to know."

"Oh . . . a lean season. Temporarily, of course. We all have them." She looked winsomely rueful. "That's a girlish secret I'm letting you in on. The difference between me and most other girls is I don't believe in staying home at these times. I go out with what comes my way, because who knows—" she batted her eyelashes "—what I might be missing, home with my pride and a good book?"

"Thank heaven for forward little girls."

"Oh, I'm not forward," she said dreamily. "Just hopeful."

"You're adorable."

"Am I?" she said, with a contented sigh. She nestled against him, adorably.

She told the nondescript next day that she just knew he'd understand how Whit, being an old friend from Denver—such an incredible coincidence—felt it only right that he should drive her back to school, having a car and being this old friend from Denver, like. The nondescript said she had no heart and no manners, at which Annabel naturally laughed, having so much of each when convenient and agreeable.

Whit continued in the laird-like pattern. He had a high-handed way of rushing a girl that Annabel, accustomed to young men too eager to please, found exciting. A spate of telephone calls and crazy little notes, unexpected arrivals at her school, then silence, then a renewal of attention . . . it kept her alert, mystified, delighted.

And so it continued through the spring. Annabel wore his class ring, with a guard, on the third finger of her left hand, but skirted questions concerning it, since she was in no position to answer them.

With Whit in one school and her in another, it was only after they got back to Denver for the summer, he to go to work in his father's firm and Annabel to give happiness by her mere presence at home, that she really began to notice this other side of him.

He was verbally as attentive as ever, protesting her a hundred vows and apparently wanting her company whenever he was free. He charmed her parents and her brother, who began to look at her meaningfully, in a way they'd not done before—Annabel being a well-known coquette and so not to be taken seriously. Her mother commented from time to time about how nice it was that Whit also came from Denver and was going into his father's business when he graduated the following year. Once or twice Annabel heard her father muttering a sentence that contained the word "intentions." Her brother asked her right out what she was waiting for, and did she think she could do better?

"Mother, make him stop," Annabel had cried out. "What does everyone *want* of me?"

"We want you to have and do whatever you want, dear," Mrs. Browning said, with a frown for her son that closed the subject, for the moment. But, as Annabel said, whether or not it was voiced, they were all waiting for her to take off the class ring and make room for the diamond. Whit's diamond.

By now Annabel was head over heels in love, who had never before done other than bow slightly to its power. She wanted Whit, wanted for the first time in her life to know and be with one man only. She wanted to be married to him. But although she wore his ring, and although she was an expert at convincing herself that what she wanted to be true was, in fact, the truth, she could not feel that they were engaged, since he hadn't asked her in words.

"What *had* he said in words?" I burst in, too desperate to keep silent.

"He said he wanted me to wear his ring," she replied crisply, "forever. Which certainly means an engagement in most cases. But with Whit . . . well, it's hard to be sure, with him, what means what."

"I know," I said without thinking.

"What?"

"I mean, I know what you mean. Generally speaking." My lips felt stiff, but I got the words out.

Annabel considered for a moment, then nodded. "As far as actually asking me to marry him," she said with wide-eyed candor and that self-deprecating expression of hers, "he made a lot of splashing noises, but never really *swam* anywhere, if you know what I mean."

"I know," I said again.

This time she ignored me, going on with her tale in an almost bemused way, as if she still couldn't credit it. I was having trouble myself. That man, that same Whit, had told me in a voice shaking with emotion that until he knew me he'd only been going through the motions of living. And I? Oh, I had answered in kind, so close to meaning it that possibly I meant it.

I looked at Annabel's beautiful profile and listened to her soft, revealing voice, and began to tell myself that, after all, he might have wearied of that superficial loveliness covering layers of little but self-regard. Wasn't it perfectly plausible to think that when he met me he knew that the past had been a mistake? Maybe he'd been afraid to tell me, for fear of losing me. Poor Whit, I said to myself, broodingly, and felt tenderness begin to melt the chill within me. Poor Whit . . . you might have trusted me. I put my hand up and touched the ring through my blouse, as though in reassurance.

"And so," Annabel was saying, "that's how it went. No place. Practically until August. Never in my life have I known a man who could talk around and around the point without ever getting anywhere near it the way Whit Larsen can."

My hand fell away. It was on the second of August, on a hot afternoon when his father had let the stenographic pool out early, that Whit had fallen into step beside me and said, "Your way is my way, and if you dispute it, there's no telling what I'll do, but it'll be drastic, rely on that."

I stopped and stared up at him, prepared, despite the attractions I'd observed closely enough to catalog, to be cool in dismissal. I've never much cared for glib people. I'm suspicious of their too easy words, their oversimplified emotions. It was this quality of glibness that put me off Annabel when we roomed together, and its presence was in Whit's tone that afternoon. But when I looked at him, I could see nothing of it in his face. It was an ingenuous, *sweet* face, and I went down before it like a reed in a morning breeze.

Annabel was still talking, and might have been stating a case for the two of us. She said that, despite his presence and his protestations, she was feeling nowhere. And then that other habit of his either got more pronounced or she began to notice it more.

He'd be with her, but not with her, as she trenchantly

put it. Beside her, and talking, always talking, a very loving game, his eyes would travel and rove, as if seeking something. Or someone. Dancing, she'd feel that he was gazing over her shoulder, sending his searching eyes everywhere, looking into every face but hers. He'd break off mid-sentence to follow a girl's figure down the street, across a room. And yet, since a murmur would recall him, regain all his attention and appeal, she'd tell herself that she was being oversensitive, that he was handsome and vigorous and full of curiosity, that such a man could not be expected to act tamed and bridled at all times. For one thing, women wouldn't let him.

"Besides," she said to me plaintively, "he told me over and over that I was all he lived for, that there'd never been anyone but me and never could be. If a man keeps saying those things, you believe him, don't you?"

I did, I said silently.

By now, in what I consider an understandable effort to soothe my own vanity, I was telling myself that I'd never really loved him. I'd been dazzled and delighted, but, after all, I'd scarcely known him a month. Not long enough to fall irrevocably in love. I suppose, to tell the truth, I was too outraged to be hurt. Annabel had known him longer. And that, I explained to my wounded ego, is why she's still thinking about him, why she's still hurt, poor girl. I felt almost condescending. Though somewhere in me something was being hurt, too, I refused to give it my attention. We save ourselves in what way we can.

"So now," I said, thinking we'd do well to get on another topic, any other topic, "here we are, on our way back, and it's all over, and really, Annabel, aren't you better off this way? I mean, you might have *married* him. Then where would you have been?"

Annabel put her gloved hands to her face and shivered a little. "Yes," she said, in a queer, flat voice, "then where would I have been?" She took her hands away, exhaled a long breath, and said, "Do you want to know what happened? I mean, what finally finished it?"

"If you want to tell me," I said gently. I was gripping the ring now, holding it away from my heart.

"His father imported some saris from India. They came in the last week of July. And one afternoon Whit came around with one. For me. It was . . . ravishing. A sort of peacock and paler blue silk. Just beautiful. You know something, Frances? He gave me this blue silk sari and said the minute he saw it, he knew it was for me. It was to go with my eyes, he said."

She turned and fixed on me her enormous, liquid, dark brown eyes. "Mother tells me women have gotten divorced for less," she said, and burst into tears.

After a while she went into the ladies' room, haughtily ignoring the curious gaze of a few people around us. While she was gone I eased the ring out of my blouse, unhooked the clasp of the thin gold chain. I held them in my palm a moment, and then dropped them, with a very final gesture, into the depths of my bag. Of course, I'd have to fish them out again later and send them to Whit, but for me the renunciation was there on the plane.

When Annabel came back she was looking fine. Pretty and flippant and in command of herself. That's the way she looks whenever I see her now, which isn't often, but we do run across one another from time to time. We've never mentioned Whit again, and I presume she's gotten over him. I know I have. It's just a matter of keeping his face, with that frank, sweet expression he had, out of mind. A matter of reminding myself not to remember his voice, or the way he'd put his hand on mine as if to say, "It's all right, I'm here."

I mean, I might have *married* him, and then where would I have been?

Storm
Under Glass

Suds Murphy leaned against a tree on the broad lawn surrounding the high school, looking quite like his name. His woolly sweater was white and emblazoned with the school letter, his hair looked like chips of yellow laundry soap, and his whole strong length looked like sun and air. One hand was in his pocket, the other held a book, which he slapped idly against his leg. His eyes remained fixed upon the leaf-embroidered grass.

Two freshmen girls passing in the outbound stream of students paid him their tribute of a glance among many glances, to which the accustomed Suds, wrapped in private considerations, paid no heed.

"*Golly,*" said the first freshman, new to town, "who is that?"

"Why, Suds Murphy, that's all," said the second freshman in a tone that said of course Suds Murphy *was* all.

"He's a senior, I guess," the first freshman sighed.

"Well, of course. Can't you tell that just by looking?"

The first freshman nodded, scuffled through a pile of

gold and russet leaves, and dreamed of distant glories—
seniors like Suds Murphy.

"He's the best shortstop in school and captain of the
football team and the best fancy diver we have and . . ."

"Oh stop," moaned the first freshman. "Stop, you're
killing me."

They went on, past the unperceiving object of their
rapture. Toward them came a red-haired girl, tiny and
ebullient, turning a delicate face and sparkling eyes up
to a dark-haired, white-sweatered-lettered boy who idled
beside her, half smiling as she burbled along to him in a
high, crackling, rather sweet voice. The first freshman
saw her eyes skim quickly toward the preoccupied Suds,
then back to the boy beside her. Her animation increased
as she neared Suds, like a lamp that leaped and fluttered.

"That's his girl friend, Audrey Hooker," the second
freshman said knowledgeably.

"Whose girl friend?" asked the first freshman, eyeing
the redhead's companion and thinking that grammar
school was never like this.

"Suds Murphy's, of course. Who are we talking about,
anyway?"

"She doesn't act it. Who's that with her?"

The two of them looked at the girl who was presum-
ably Suds's, and at the boy beside her. To the first freshman it seemed outrageously unfair that one girl should be
in apparent possession of two such heroes. Then she decided that after all it was a good sign. If one girl could do
it, why so could another—in a couple of years, naturally.

The first freshman was pretty.

"Who's with her?" she repeated.

"That's Dick Perine. He's captain of the track team, plays center on the basketball team, is the . . ."

The first freshman shook her head. "It's too much." They walked along slowly, looking back now and then. "Whose girl *is* she?"

"Suds Murphy's, I said. Only . . . only she's a vampire. She can't stop collecting men. *And* she's always trying to make Suds jealous. She's the disgrace of the high school," the second freshman announced primly.

The first freshman decided then and there that her one purpose was to become a disgrace by senior year. "Does he?" she asked. "Get jealous, I mean."

The other shrugged. "Why should he? Look at him."

The first freshman had looked. She thought probably Suds wouldn't have to get jealous, but you can't tell.

They went around a corner and disappeared, unremarked.

Suds, intently studying the green ground beneath him, felt, without looking up, the approach of Audrey and Dick, and within him something hurtful tumbled as hectically as the dry brilliant leaves tumbled through the air around him. Here it was, only October, and she was up to her tricks again. Just last week he'd held her very tight in his arms and listened to her whispered, almost lisped, "Oh, Sudsy, you know it's only you. You *know*." And he had known. In a way, he knew it now. But that was Audrey. She just couldn't stop looking around.

It was like that darn poem of Browning's they were studying. A poem Suds couldn't understand very easily, but which had imprinted itself in his mind because of a few lines. Mr. Owen, the English teacher, had read it aloud, and when he came to those lines, Suds had sat up abruptly. That's Audrey, he said to himself. Browning might just as well have been writing about Audrey. He'd gone home and memorized the lines.

" 'She had a heart—how shall I say?—too soon made glad,
Too easily impressed; she liked whate'er
She looked on, and her looks went everywhere.' "

Suds muttered the lines over to himself. I ought to print them on a card and hang it on her back, he thought. People have written poems about you, Audrey, he told her silently as she and Dick approached. Did you know that, Aud? Except I guess maybe you wouldn't like the poem too much, he added with gratification.

"Hi, Suds," said Dick. "How's the boy? You look pretty bored."

"Medium tedium," Suds agreed. He glanced at Audrey and his heart rolled over like an obedient dog. Oh, pretty, flippant, flirty Audrey. So awfully, awfully pretty. "Hello, Audrey," he said casually.

Audrey smiled and swung a little, hands behind her back, like a girl in calico and bonnet. "Lo, Sudsy. Where've you been? Dick and I have been looking everywhere."

"I'll bet."

Audrey smiled with delight. When she smiled, she sort of bit her lower lip a little. Suds thought it was enchanting. So did a lot of other people, he realized glumly.

Dick turned away, with a sidelong glance at Audrey that looked as if it spoke volumes, but probably, Suds assured himself, didn't mean a darn thing. Dick was sort of handy with the long soulful glances. He and Audrey were a pair, all right.

"So long, you two," Dick said benignly.

"Bye, Dick," Audrey said on a lingering note.

Suds bobbed his head, and Dick strode off.

They stood in a silence during which Suds tried to calm the storm that always rose in him at the sight, at the very thought, of Audrey. Lord, he thought, girls get away with so much, just by being pretty. Because here he was, just about the biggest man in the school, he thought simply, and look what this girl could do to him.

Suds, who would admit that his mind was not precisely razor sharp, was sharp enough to realize that almost any girl in the school would drop whatever she was doing and come on the run if he just gave the word. It wasn't vanity. Just fact. After three years of this sort of adulation, he could hardly not recognize it.

"Dick's been asking me to the Autumn Dance," Audrey said with a swift uplifting of her lovely eyes that she knew melted Suds like an icicle in a bonfire.

Suds frowned and a sudden anger possessed him. What the heck did she think she was doing? She knew she was going to that dance with him, not with Dick or anyone else. What sort of a girl was she, anyway? He got so angry that a brilliant retort occurred to him, one that would never have entered his usual easygoing mind.

"That's fine," he said. "You ought to have a good time with Dick."

Audrey gasped a little. She turned her head, started to smile, stopped. "Why, Sudsy," she breathed softly. "Why, Sudsy."

Suds retained a strong grip on his emotions and said nothing. This time he was going to teach her. Around them the students came and went in noisy converging and disintegrating groups. Most of the girls looked wistfully at Suds, the boys rather speculatively at Audrey. But no one spoke to them. The twisting flaming leaves tossed in a mild breeze, and Suds, realizing that his only safety lay in silence, remained in it.

Audrey put out a hand, laid it lightly on Suds's wool-covered arm. She pressed, ever so lightly, to show that she liked his muscles. Suds stared over her head, waiting to be released.

"Sudsy?" she said in a husky plea. "Don't be mad. I didn't say yes to him."

So you didn't say no, either? thought the boy achingly. He'd been almost ready to capitulate, but that did it. "Well, you've got plenty of time left," he said and gently removed her detaining hand. "So long, Audrey. See you around."

He walked away from her quickly, not looking back till he'd crossed the broad lawn to a little thicket of trees.

Then he turned, hoping rather desperately that she'd be following, or even watching. But in the mass of people he saw no sign of her fiery hair, her yellow-green sweater. He'd know Audrey at any distance, and she wasn't there.

With a sigh he sank to the ground, leaning against the bole of a tree, fixing his eyes without focus on the grass that was turning a sort of yellow-green, like Aud's sweater.

In spite of his torment, he knew underneath that it would work out. He and Audrey would go to the dance together, as they'd planned. Because Aud was really his girl, and they both knew it. But he had to teach her a lesson. He thought if this kept up he wouldn't be able to concentrate on football, let alone the various things he had to study for school in order to get to college and play football.

But how to do it? Audrey was probably a little dumfounded right now by his behavior, but she wouldn't be for long. She had the slickest way of calling him back to her side by doing absolutely nothing. For a moment he had a hideous picture of her, right now, telling Dick that she *would* go to the dance with him. If she were angry enough, she might do that. Firmly he pushed the thought away. Because, to begin with, Audrey never got angry. He'd never seen her even slightly ruffled. And, to go on with—he took a deep breath—to go on with, there was the matter of pride. He did have some, whether or not she thought so, and it would darn well stand by him if by any chance she should decide to go with Dick.

He felt utterly miserable, and in a little while he'd

just have to get going for football practice. He was already late, but for once it didn't seem to matter. A few minutes wasn't going to kill anyone. Oh, darn you, Audrey, he thought. Going around liking whatever you look on, and looking everywhere. Darn you, anyway.

But the thing is, he went on to himself, the thing is to give her a real lesson. Once she got really scared, then he wouldn't have to put up with this sort of thing any more. A lesson. Well, obviously it would have to be another girl. Competition is the only thing Audrey would understand, he decided with sad comprehension. Briefly his mind flicked over the possibilities. There were plenty of girls around, and he knew any of them would be glad of a chance to give Aud one in the eye. He grinned a little. Quite a girl, she was, his Audrey.

But after a few arduous moments of concentration he shook his head. The trouble was that most of the girls were so darn much like Audrey, only less so. She'd catch on like a flash if he suddenly started dating any of them. It was all dismally difficult. He sighed again, hugely, and lifted his eyes from the autumn grass.

And solved his problem.

Away across the lawn, about fifty feet from Suds, and not noticing him, was Jenny Barnard. She sat on a bench, studying. Suds didn't recall ever having noticed her very much, but he knew right away who she was. A very quiet sort of girl, new this year, who never appeared much in evidence around the school, but who somehow was quite obviously not a drip. A drip would never do for his purpose, but a girl like Jenny Barnard, who was, he decided now, pretty in a different sort of way, might do excellently. Audrey would never understand why he'd be dating this sort of girl, and it would get her thinking.

He looked Jenny Barnard over very carefully. Nice figure. Her hair was longish, almost to her shoulders. That by itself made her different. Suds thought that most of the girls these days looked like they'd gotten crew cuts. And then, with a catch at his heart, thought of Audrey's short flaming curls that lay against her head like a glistening Dutch cap. With an effort, he turned again to the matter of Jenny Barnard. Well, long hair, nice figure. She seemed to be dressed more or less like all the others, but she was—stiller. She didn't pull at her hair, nor drag out a pack of cigarettes and puff nervously, nor fiddle with her hands. Just sat there, reading.

She'll do, he decided. With the simple confidence of one who has never been refused, he decided to start dating her. Obviously, since she'd never showed up at any of the games or dances, or at least not to his knowledge, she'd be glad of a chance to start going places with Suds Murphy. It would, he thought magnanimously, make all the difference in the world to her socially.

Suds was a kindly person and had made all the difference in the world to several girls, at dances and things like that. Not the hopeless ones, but girls just teetering on the edge of acceptance. Suds would look around at a dance, spot such a one and cut in. After that, she was made, even if he never said more than "Hi" to her again as they met in the halls. With an utter lack of vanity, he was aware of this prerogative of his, and used it well.

He got up, seeing that Jenny Barnard was closing her book, and strolled over.

"Hi, Jenny," he said casually.

Jenny Barnard glanced up, blinked in unmasked surprise and smiled. "Oh, hello—Suds." She collected her things, stood up. Suds thought she moved well. It pleased him.

"Where're you off to?" he asked, falling into step beside her.

"Home."

"Where's home?"

"Over that way," said Jenny, waving a hand in the general direction of past the football field, but not specifying an address.

"Well then, I'm going your way," Suds said with a smile. When she didn't reply, he added, "That is, if it's okay with you."

Jenny nodded. "That would be nice."

She wasn't exactly turning handsprings, but Suds found that more pleasing than otherwise. You couldn't fool Aud with a pushover.

He and Jenny walked along rather slowly. She seemed content to have his company, but didn't plead for his conversation. Suds hardly noticed their silence, so occupied was he with this budding plan. In a way, he thought, it was slightly unfair to Jenny here, because of course he couldn't take her to the Autumn Dance and she might get the idea that he would. But, as before, he solaced his conscience with the knowledge that his interest would probably induce some other fellow to ask her.

"I'll have to leave you at the football field," he said after a while. "I'm late for practice now."

"That's right. You're captain, aren't you?"

Suds glanced at her suspiciously. All very well to pretend indifference, that was part of a girl's game. But it could be carried too far. Everyone, he thought with innocent self-esteem, knew he played end and was captain of the team. But her face showed an even more than normal interest in his answer. Almost, he thought warily, almost as if she were—pretending interest. A second's thought assured him that such a thing was patently impossible. The poor girl was just so unused to the important "clicks"—he pronounced the word in his mind—that she didn't know quite what to say.

He nodded. "Yup. You don't get to the games much, do you?"

"Oh, no. Not here. That is—I'm usually so busy weekends," she said hastily.

Suds was a bit disappointed. If there was any type of girl he liked less than the determinedly "intellectual" one, it was the one who pretended to be up to her collarbone in dates when anyone could see she wasn't. Even up to her toenails. He wondered if perhaps he'd misunderstood and decided to give her another chance. Of course tomorrow night, Friday, he had a regular date with Audrey—only what was he going to do about it? He sighed, knowing darn well he'd show up on her porch on schedule. But tonight—well, tonight he'd give her a scare. Not phone, not appear. He'd take Jenny out.

"You busy tonight?" he asked.

Jenny looked up at him with a little smile. She really did have a nice face. Sort of oval and—what would the word be?—sort of serene, Suds decided. "Yes, I am," she said.

Suds, who'd anticipated her answer so firmly that he didn't listen to it, said, "Well, in that case, could I come over to your house? We could take in a movie, or . . ."

"Suds," she said. "You didn't hear. I *am* busy tonight."

The boy stopped walking. Quite simply, since he'd begun to ask girls out at all, he'd not had a single refusal, and with a history like that he was now left with nothing to say. He looked so completely astonished that Jenny began to laugh.

"It's a shame," she assured him, not sounding in the least sorry. "I'm going to the theater with my parents."

Suds just about groaned. The "theater"! Why couldn't she say movie and let it go at that? He was beginning to think the whole thing was a bad idea. Audrey was his sort of girl, and he missed her already. A cute, saucy girl who didn't have to put on airs. She's got so many naturally, he thought, half proudly, half irritatedly. Maybe if she had a few less, he wouldn't be in this silly predicament now, asking a girl who never had dates for a date she wouldn't accept. His pride, a delicate instrument that had been harshly used today, suddenly rebelled.

"Well, my gosh," he burst out. "If you tell your parents —I mean, wouldn't they understand—if you found something you'd rather do? I mean . . ." He was flushed and almost incoherent. The conceit he had was not innate, it had been pressed upon him by success. It stood now in danger of disintegrating completely at a first setback.

Jenny shook her head. "I wouldn't rather. That sounds impolite, Suds. But, truly, Dad got tickets for this play ages ago, and we do want to go." Her voice was extremely gentle. "I'd have liked it, otherwise," she added after a moment of studying his face.

"Oh. A play. I thought you meant . . . I see." Suds subsided, and they walked on. "I guess I sounded pretty conceited. But of course you want to go to the play." He nodded his head to indicate how thoroughly he understood.

They had reached the football field by now and Suds slowed up at the gate. "Jenny," he said, with a sudden decision. "How about tomorrow night? Are you busy then?" This is going to decide it, one way or the other, he told himself. Audrey would be mad enough to skin him, but the importance of getting a date with Jenny seemed uppermost right now. He owed it to his pride, as well as his plan. "Could you?" he asked again. Imagine—Suds Murphy, practically on his knees for a date. He waited for her answer in a mixture of anxiety and amazement. When she nodded, he almost, not quite, sighed with relief.

"Oh, fine," he said robustly, and then lowered his voice. "Like to go over to the 'Dream Den' and dance? I can't stay out too late, of course. Training. But we could cut a scatter rug." That didn't sound too funny after he'd said it. But you can't be witty every time.

"That would be nice." She gave him a quick smile and turned to go.

"Hey, Jenny," he shouted, and was aware of several of the boys on the field and a few visiting girls looking over at the sound of his voice. This'll do it, he thought gleefully. Aud will know now.

"You forgot to give me your address," he told the girl.

At eight thirty the next night Suds rang the bell at the door of a neat white house and was greeted at the door by Jenny. She looked pretty but not spectacular. Suds, used to Audrey's extra-specialness on date nights, was disappointed. You'd think a girl could fix herself up—a fluffy blouse, trick heels, bows in her hair, something or other. Jenny wore a black wool dress and a few gold bracelets, neat black shoes with low heels. But her hair gleamed and her lips had a nice color.

She led the way to a large living room. It had dark green walls, a white mantel and thick rugs. It was covered from ceiling to floor and wall to wall with bookcases. Full of books. There was a large desk near a window. It was littered with papers that looked suspiciously and unpleasantly like theme papers to Suds.

From behind the desk a grayish tall man rose with outstretched hand. Jenny's mother was sitting in a wing chair. She smiled warmly and casually at Suds as he was introduced.

He settled uneasily on the edge of a couch. Meetings

with parents were never free of worry for him, because he wasn't entirely sure of his manners. He stared at the cannel-coal fire, thinking that the room was very fine and rather like a library. It made him respectful, and that in turn made him uncomfortable, so that his usual ready flow of words dried up. Besides, he had a peculiar feeling of outsideness. With Audrey or the other girls he knew, there was generally an indefinable aligning of parents on one side, Suds and the girl on the other. Nothing too noticeable, and certainly not unexpected. Here it almost seemed as though these three were on the other side, and he alone. He realized that they would never expect or intend it to be so. But Jenny was comfortable with her parents where Aud was always a bit nervous about hers.

Suds fidgeted, addressed Mr. Barnard as "Sir" and wished he were with Audrey.

Mr. Barnard waved at his desk. "Doing my homework," he explained with a sigh.

Suds smiled and made an easy guess. "You're a teacher, sir?"

Jenny's father nodded. "English literature."

It didn't surprise Suds at all that Jenny's father should turn out to be teaching the least attractive subject of all. He seemed to be running into that sort of luck lately. "We're on Browning," he said in a tone that brought a smile to Mr. Barnard's face. " 'How They Brought the Good News from Ghent to Aix,' " the boy brooded. He looked up suddenly. "What's he talking about? What news? Who brought it?" He lifted his shoulders. "I don't get Browning, sir. I think a book of instructions oughta go with him."

Mr. Barnard laughed. "You aren't alone in that." But he made no attempt to explain, and for that Suds was grateful.

The boy's eyes strayed back to the desk. There was a large round paperweight on it. The thick glass kind, with a little figure of a deer lying beneath an evergreen on the bottom. Suds brightened. He liked those things. "Does that make a snowstorm?" he inquired, getting up.

Mrs. Barnard said it did. "We're awfully fond of it."

"I like them too," Suds told her, unaware of his own lessening tension. He picked it up. The glass was heavy and cool. It made a satisfying roundness in the palm of his hand. Gently he turned it over, turned it back. The whirling snow spun in a wild white fracas, settling and sifting slowly on the tiny green tree, the little alert deer. They all watched till the last few flakes had spiraled to rest.

"That's the way a storm should be," Suds mused. "Under glass." He put the paperweight down, glanced over at the Barnards to find them all looking at him with a very obvious and warming interest. It pleased him, but he didn't know what could have caused it.

In the car, on their way to the Dream Den, Suds asked, "Where does your father teach?"

"Yale."

"Oh."

He couldn't think of a thing to add. Somehow he'd

assumed Mr. Barnard taught at one of the schools in town. The town was a sort of suburb of New Haven, easily commutable. He was impressed by the information, as he was always impressed by people whose brains seemed busier and more capable than average. Thinking it over, he wondered suddenly if what Jenny had meant by her hesitation yesterday when he talked of football was that she went to college games only. Unreasonably, irrepressibly, he became annoyed.

"You go to the football games with your parents, like you go to the theater?" he asked shortly.

Jenny took a moment to answer. Then, "Sometimes," she said.

"No wonder you can't be bothered with our games."

"It isn't that, Suds. I just don't seem to . . . I don't know many people around the school—"

"Whose fault is that?" he interrupted. He was quite aware of how he sounded, and quite unable to stop sounding so. The fact that she answered so gently only increased his irritation. Everything about her was too darn assured. Her background, her manners, the things she didn't say. He decided that of course she only went out with college men. He decided her black dress was probably in better taste than Aud's funny little ribbons and ruffly things.

Oh, Aud, he cried in his mind. Aud, *I love you.* What was he doing with this girl anyway? His plan, that marvelous plan that seemed so smart yesterday, was nothing but a bitter taste in his mouth tonight. And where was Audrey now? He had a sudden picture of her, sitting home waiting for his call, his knock at the door. He saw her so clearly, sitting in her living room that was practically like his own, with plain colored walls and a couple of books on a table, propped up between elephant bookends. He thought all this while the sound of his own words, "Whose fault is that?" was still in his ears.

"It isn't anyone's fault at all," she said. "It's just the way things work out sometimes. We lived in New Haven until last May, and I just sort of got in the habit . . ." She stopped, went on again. "I knew some boys who went to Yale this year, and . . ."

"What're you explaining to me for?" Suds asked unfairly.

Jennie sighed a little, and they pulled into the parking lot beside the Dream Den.

Audrey wasn't sitting home beside the elephant bookends. She was whirling over the waxed dance floor under a paper-lanterned ceiling in the capable arms of Dick Perine. She wore a green velvet skirt, a white blouse, a wreath of little white and green flowers in her bright hair. Her small feet skipped over the floor in green high-heeled sandals. Suds, at the doorway, saw her immediately. She looks . . . adorable, he thought. He recognized that his thought was defensive for her, but the old familiar rumpus began in his heart. The stormy reaction that the sight of Audrey always brought. She certainly didn't waste any time, he muttered to himself.

Jenny, strangely quiet even for her, walked beside Suds to a table, where they ordered Cokes and then sat staring at each other. It occurred to Suds that he was managing to make her evening about as uncomfortable as he possibly could. At the same time he reluctantly conceded that she was being nicer about it than he could have imagined possible. Probably, he told himself, because she doesn't give a darn. She's sitting there telling herself that it will all be over soon and she'll have the comfort of having been a perfect lady. Never in his eighteen years had Suds felt so confused, so dissatisfied with himself.

"Dance?" he said woodenly.

Dancing with Jenny was like dancing with a wing—like skimming about with your own shadow. Suds, who loved dancing, began to smile a little. He put away all his thoughts. He just simply danced with Jenny.

Later—how much later?—when they were back at the table, Suds glanced up as Dick and Audrey made for the door. Audrey turned and gave him one long bewildered look of pure pain. Then she lifted her head a little, laughed up at Dick and disappeared. Suds stared at the empty doorway, thinking without any triumph, without much feeling at all, that his plan had certainly worked. But it wasn't a very good plan. It hadn't solved anything.

For three or four days after that, Suds avoided everyone as much as he could. But he found himself looking for Jenny, in the halls, on the lawns, near the football field. He saw Audrey with Dick two or three times, and each time when her eyes met his, his habituated heart leaped attentively. But on the fourth day he went into a drugstore and called Jenny, because he couldn't stop remembering her quiet voice and the lightness of her dancing.

"Jenny, will you go to the Autumn Dance with me?" he asked, and then waited in a pounding silence. He felt disloyal, he felt miserable. But he wanted to take Jenny to the dance.

"Oh, Suds," she said, sounding really disappointed, "Suds, I'm terribly sorry, but I won't be here the weekend of the dance." When he didn't reply, she added, "Truly, I'd have loved it, if you'd asked earlier."

"Oh, that's okay, Jenny," he said finally. "I'll call again."

He hung up. He didn't want to ask where she'd be instead. Well, he'd certainly fixed things, but only for himself. Some planner. He shoved his hands in his pockets and walked out of the drugstore. It was early evening and a purple smoky dusk filled the sharp air. The drugstore windows were alight, and a red neon sign overhead. The street lamps were on. Suds sighed, a long sad sound, and started home.

"Suds?"

He turned at the familiar voice. Audrey, in a tan suede jacket, a narrow blue ribbon round her hair, stood a few feet away, looking at him uncertainly. Uncertainty in Audrey seemed so pathetic to Suds that he almost protested aloud. But all he said was, "Oh, hello, Aud," in a welcoming tone.

She moved nearer. "Sudsy?" Each time she said his name it was a question. "Where're you going?"

"Home. Where're you?"

"Home too, I guess," she sighed. "I had to come down —for aspirin. My mother has a headache," she explained, as though to apologize for being there.

"That's a shame," Suds said.

They fell into step together.

It's funny, Suds was thinking. When he looked at Aud he could feel, just like always, the rapid beating of his heart. If he looked at her hard enough he remembered all the things she used to mean to him. If he reminded himself how pretty she was, how much all the other guys liked her, how good she felt when he held her close—if he remembered all those things, he could feel the storm again that used to rise so naturally at the sight or the thought of her. A storm under glass, he thought, and a picture of Jenny in her black wool dress came into his mind with naturalness and longing.

They were almost at Audrey's house. He turned to say goodbye and swallowed painfully. Quietly, without a sound at all, Aud was crying. The tears rolled down her face and she stood, turning her head a little from side to side, not speaking.

"Aud, don't," he said softly.

"No. I won't, in a little while." She pulled out a handkerchief, wiped her eyes. "I'm awfully dumb," she said in a shaky voice. "In every way."

"No, you aren't," the boy said urgently. "Aud, you—"

"Sudsy," she interrupted. "Sudsy, you'll have to tell me. . . . Are you . . . I mean, can't we . . ." She put a hand against her head in a small desperate gesture. "Are you

70

so--gone away from me?" It seemed as if she'd used up all her strength asking that. Now she just waited.

How awful, Suds cried silently, what a horrible thing love is. To make a pretty proud girl like Audrey—so humble. He shook his head, getting Jenny out of it. "Of course not, Aud," he told her. "Of course not."

She took a deep breath. "Well, then . . . Sudsy, I told Dick I wouldn't go to the Autumn Dance with him." She waited, and then, with a peculiarly feminine air of abandoning all pride once having abandoned a little, blurted, "*Are* you going to ask me, Sudsy?"

He leaned over and kissed her fragrant hair very lightly. "Sure I am, Aud," he said. "I'm asking you now."

The Robin

Young Mrs. John MacIntyre, in her garden on an early
spring afternoon, was one of the happiest women in town,
and, what was more, she knew it, was aware each moment
of pleasure and pride and contentment. Once she leaned
her cheek against her hand and laughed a little, thinking
what Linda would say about the reasons for such happiness. "What are you crowing and glowing about?" she
had her absent sister ask with delicate arching of a slim
brow. "Oh, things," Mrs. MacIntyre replied airily. "Such
as?" the Linda of her mind persisted. "Such as my garden,
and that wash hanging over there so gaily, and the lemon
pie in on my kitchen sideboard, and it being warm and
Friday and almost time for Johnny to get home." Such a
reply was too much for Linda Powers. "Oh, my word,"
she said wearily, "how pre-feminist," and vanished from
her sister's mind.

Marion Powers MacIntyre straightened and regarded
smugly the row of fuchsia plants over which she'd worked
with inexpert devotion for most of the afternoon. You
certainly wouldn't think it would take anybody that long
to get twenty little plants arranged for summer. Of

course, she had to count the long minutes of simply leaning back to sniff the air and run loving eyes over her house, where the windows sparkled from yesterday's efforts. And part of the time she'd simply dream. She generally did. Johnny, unlike Linda and Dad, seemed to find it charming. Thinking of Johnny, she smiled again and removed her garden gloves, slapping them against her jeans. She'd get the washing in, and there'd be time for a shower before she started dinner.

It was then she saw the robin. He came springing around the side of the house, sleek and fat, with an arrogant air that seemed to say, "I may not be rare or dazzlingly beautiful, but, *heavens,* how I am loved."

Marion watched him with delight. The first robin of my marriage, she said to herself, and added, I'm daft, I really am. Or it could be spring fever. But none of her twenty-three previous springs had ever found her laughing in a garden, all alone. Until she'd married Johnny, she'd practically never been alone in her life. Dad's presence was enormous. There was Nora, their housekeeper over the years. The succession of maids. The procession of friends and acquaintances and admirers of Dad. The house had seemed at all times to be in flux, but it had certainly never seemed empty. Most of all, there had been Linda, after whom Marion had tagged from the day she'd learned to get on her two feet and point them in Linda's direction.

The robin about to bound past Marion's shining cellar window suddenly halted as he caught his reflection in the pane. He tipped his head curiously, turned and advanced upon the stranger in the glass. Marion hugged her arms with amusement as he pecked tentatively, withdrew and pecked again. The silly, silly bird, she thought, wondering what he'd do next. The little spade dangled from her fingers and the bright wash hung unattended as she watched this tiny circus in the garden. But now, in a sudden access of jealousy and frustration, the robin hurled himself at the windowpane and was dashed back onto the grass, where he lay stunned and quiet.

"Oh, *no,*" Marion said aloud.

She dropped the spade and went cautiously toward the fallen bird, who made no attempt to rise. Gently Marion took him up. In her hands he huddled warmly, his breath lifting his small body, his beak open.

"Can't you walk?" Marion asked him softly, setting him on the grass away from the window. But he slumped on splayed claws and stared ahead. She took him up again and walked around the garden looking for a likely place to set him. Not near the ground, on account of cats. Even the roof of the shed wouldn't do. The garage roof? But she'd have to have a ladder to reach it, and how could she carry the bird and a ladder too? She had a peculiar moment of wishing Linda were available, because Linda had solutions for everything. Linda did not dream and wander about, idly posing herself questions. Of course, it was farfetched to think of Linda rescuing fallen robins, but if she'd had to, an answer would have been produced immediately.

The Robin

The bird stirred in her hands and Marion looked down at it with happy encouragement. "All right, now," she coaxed. "You're fine, really." She turned her palms back, feeling the scratchy claws begin to take a purchase. The robin stretched his neck, closed his beak, suddenly fluttered away to a nearby branch, where he clung a bit dizzily before taking off on a longer flight. Marion sighed with relief. But what a silly bird, she repeated. Now there wouldn't be time to get the wash in, so it would just have to hang out all night. Maybe moonlight was good for clothes.

She had finished her shower and was fastening the bow of a fresh cotton dress when the phone rang, and Linda said, "Darling, look, I'm in a fearful rush, but can you get your things packed for a week's trip to Quebec? My treat, love."

"Huh?" said Marion. There was silence from Linda, who didn't often associate with people who said "huh?" "I mean," Marion added, "what do *you* mean?"

"I haven't much time to explain, but, essentially, I've gotten a commission to go to Quebec and sketch quaintness of all kinds. *Very* good money, so since it's your birthday next week, this is my present. We'll have a wonderful time, darling. Just like the old days—you and me. Oh, and probably Dad will make it in a few days. I told him about it and he said he'd like to be in on the birthday festivities—"

"But what about Johnny?" Marion asked curiously. There was no force in her voice. There never was when

75

she spoke to Linda, because for some reason the things you said to Linda always seemed a bit superfluous. Yet Linda was sweet, and generous. You could not blame her for forgetting that husbands must be fed and . . . remained with, so to speak. Linda, dashing from one assignment to the next, never thought of food till she picked up the menu, and didn't need to stay with anyone, being quite completely free.

"Johnny?" Linda echoed. "Oh, but, love, much as I'd like to include him," she said without troubling to sound truthful, "I just could not afford it. Anyway, doesn't he have to work?"

"Of course he has to work. That's what I mean. I just can't pack and take off this way. He eats, you know. And there's the housework." And my garden, she added to herself, knowing it would sound like no reason at all to Linda. People didn't, according to Linda, allow themselves to be *tied* by things. A garden would sound like the lamest excuse in the world, but surely even Linda— once she'd remembered about Johnny—would realize that her offer was quite impossible.

Linda realized nothing of the sort. "Well, but, good heavens, can't he manage without you for a few days? He managed for years, you know."

"That was before we were married."

"Yes."

They were just not understanding each other, Marion thought, beginning to feel unhappy. She hated to hurt her sister, but their worlds were so far apart now. Linda, living in the city, working all over the world. Marion, living in the suburbs, working in a six-room house and a sixty-foot garden. A year ago, Marion thought, neither of us knew what a Launderette was, and now it's as familiar to me as . . . as the A&P is. She giggled at that.

Linda, taking the giggle for pleasure, laughed happily. "Oh, well, fine," she said. "It's settled. Can you come in early tomorrow? Then we could shop. The plane goes Sunday morning."

"Wait," Marion said. "Wait, Linda. Please, honey—" She could hear Linda's intaken breath. "I mean, *darling*." Did that sound a little acid? "I'd adore it, Linda, truly. But I just can't announce to Johnny that I'm leaving for a week. And, anyway, I think he'd like me to be with *him* on my birthday." I know darn well he would.

"Well, I never *heard* anything so dreary," Linda said with bewilderment. "Can't a man . . . I mean, after all, I'm not asking you to get a divorce. I'm asking you accept a short vacation, as my gift. Could he really be that unreasonable? Johnny has certainly never struck me as a selfish person—" In the urgency of the moment she was prepared to concede Johnny a virtue. "How in the world do we know when I'll be able to do a thing like this again? Besides," she added wistfully, "I did so count on it, Marion. Please."

Marion shook her head unhappily, but, in spite of herself, felt the old wish to please, above all, this loved and brilliant sister. The old desire to be as much like her as possible—dashing and glamorous. It was a need she'd had

77

long before she'd needed Johnny. It was what had led her to dress like Linda, imitate Linda's inflections and expressions, follow Linda to art school.

"I'd have to think it over," she said slowly.

"All right," her sister answered without expression.

"Don't, please don't be angry. You can't be expected to understand, you or Dad." She sounded apologetic. "It's just that—"

"That what?" Linda prompted.

Marion sighed. Just that when you're married, you stay with your husband. You don't say, "Here, dear, manage by yourself and I'll be back in a week." Linda would understand that no more than she had ever really understood Marion's marriage to begin with. "I don't know. Could I call you in the morning?"

"Of course."

But Linda was hurt now. And Marion, going to the kitchen, was hurt too. It was, as Dad would say, a woeful dilemma. And, after all, what was wrong with the idea? A little time away from each other might be good for her and Johnny. All the marriage counselors advised it. At least, she had the impression that they did. A healthy change. Since she and Johnny had only been married several months, a healthy change was not imperative yet, but there wasn't anything wrong in the wish to take advantage of Linda's marvelous offer. And they *would* have fun. It had been wonderful in New Orleans that time, wandering around while Linda's white sketch pad came to life with delicate garden scenes, fountains, old cast-iron grille work, restaurants and street scenes. That had also been a present from Linda. And last year, when a fashion magazine had sent Linda to Italy to do a series of sketches in Florence and Rome, Marion had again been invited.

"But I can't do that," she said to Linda and Dad. "I mean, I have a job now." No one had taken Marion's job very seriously, not even Marion. Being a full-time artist in a department store appeared in a pretty dim light besides Linda's brilliant free-lancing. Still, she didn't want to discard a hard-won position (she'd climbed past toasters and washrags to arrive at the title of fashion artist) even to share the fruits of Linda's abilities. "I can't afford it," she said stubbornly.

"Now, puss," Dad had said. "Now, puss." Which meant, naturally, that he would underwrite her part of the trip. Dad, famous as a casual but incisive essayist and a fiercely unpleasable drama critic, could easily send a daughter off to Italy in style.

"Don't now puss me," Marion said, with unexpected spirit. "Perhaps my job doesn't mean much to you and Linda, but it means something to me. Can't you let me alone with it long enough to see if I'm any good?"

"You don't have to curl over an easel in a drawing factory to prove anything to us," Linda said. "We know you're good, darling. It's just that it would be so much more fun for me to have you along. And fun for you too, I should think," she added hastily.

"Oh . . . fun." They didn't realize that she wasn't trying to prove something to them, but to herself. "I'm working on the resort catalog. I can't just drop it in the middle, can I?"

Linda shrugged, that graceful easy shrug which was so much a part of her character. "If that's more important than I am . . ."

"Oh, Linda, I didn't mean that," Marion said anxiously. She couldn't bear these recessions of Linda's, these hurt withdrawals. "Darling, I'll see what I can do. Maybe I'll be able to actually finish before you—we—have to leave."

Dad had closed his eyes briefly. "All that careful schooling," he said in a mournful tone, "and she still splits infinitives."

The next day Marion approached Mrs. Eastman, the copywriter and her superior. "Mrs. Eastman—"

"Oh, there you are. Look, dear, call down to Lingerie and have them send that negligee up, yes? I want that two-page undie spread by Friday. Tell them we've *got* to have it. No buts from that dictatoress down there. Tell them I said so, yes?"

"Yes," Marion said dryly.

The lingerie buyer, Miss Brown, was a woman of difficult temperament, and the merest hint that you wanted something she was in a position to refuse was enough to make her dig in her heels and protest loudly that you were lousing up her whole department with such an outrageous request. Marion was generally able to get around her, unhappily aware that it was the Powers name that worked magic. I should have taken a disguise, she told herself peevishly, reaching for the phone. Probably I'd still be on toasters, but think how honest I'd feel.

"Miss Brown? This is . . . this is the art department. We'd like to have that blue negligee . . . you know. We're doing the two-page spread, and—"

"Now look, dearie. For you I'd let the thing go up. But it's a sample, see? And I promised the manufacturer I wouldn't let it out of my sight, but not of my *sight*."

"But—"

"No buts," Miss Brown said firmly. There was a terrible amount of noise in the background, and the buyer had to yell to be heard. Marion moved the phone away a few inches.

"That's what Mrs. Eastman says."

"How's that?"

"Mrs. Eastman also says no buts. And I still need the negligee." Marion added loudly, "What's all that racket?"

"They're redoing the department. *Again.* Fluted pink walls, plaster angels, mauve rugs. Now, I ask you—"

"Miss Brown? What am I going to do?"

A pause, and then, "Well, tell you what. Why don't you come down here and sketch the model? That way we'll maybe have a little peace from everybody."

Peace, echoed Marion when she arived at Lingerie, which was bravely struggling to carry on business in spite of a piercing buzz-saw, a battalion of carpenters and electricians. Signs in graceful script informed the customers that their indulgence would be amply rewarded by a magnificent new department in which it would be more than ever delightful to clothe the intimate woman. Marion skirted her way through sawhorses and woodshavings, sidestepped to avoid a board passing on a burly shoulder, and fell over a length of cable.

"Oh, for Pete's sake," she snapped, examining first her drawing board and then her stockings.

"Can't you get up?"

She lifted her face to the man who spoke. He grinned when he saw she was merely assessing minor damages, and put out a hand to help. Mechanically taking it, she was lifted to her feet with ease and strength.

"Gosh, thanks," she murmured, brushing off her skirt, and became abruptly conscious that she hadn't taken her eyes off his once since he'd spoken. Flushing, she began to back off.

"Hey, look out," he said with a laugh, and pulled her out of the way of yet another passing board.

"It's dangerous here," she said plaintively, and smiled too.

"Isn't it? Good thing I was on hand."

Cheeky, she thought. But—attractive as sin. That was a Linda expression. Tall, with dark hair and eyes. He wore his jeans and blue shirt like a cavalier, and continued to look at her silently, with flagrant approval.

"Well," Marion said in confusion. "Well . . . thanks again." She turned away, walked squarely into Miss Brown, and could feel him laughing behind her. "Here I am, Miss Brown," she said clearly.

"I could hardly miss you, dearie. Over this way."

Marion, following Miss Brown's undulant walk, couldn't resist a quick backward glance. And yes, he was watching her. He gave a smile and a small wave of encouragement. Because I haven't stumbled over anything for five seconds, she thought. She felt a peculiar warmth at interpreting his thoughts.

"Who's that?" she asked Miss Brown, and wished she hadn't.

"Who's who?"

"Never mind."

They entered another, less noisy section, apart from the sales department, where the blue negligee fell in exquisite folds over the body of an exquisite wax mannequin. "Well, it *is* pretty," she said.

"Divine," Miss Brown said sharply. "So, I'll leave you to it. The rest of the stuff can go upstairs. You tell that hoity-toity copywriter up there that the layout is not to be changed in any way from what I indicated." Miss Brown anticipated trouble from Mrs. Eastman, but, before she left, took care that Marion knew no blame attached to her. "Don't mind me, Miss Powers. I know *you* do the best you can. How are your father and sister, dear?"

"Fine. Dad's—"

"Such genius people. I follow your sister's work *faith*fully. What she's doing for Christaman's line is a wonder. Those wonderful sketches. And does she think of the captions underneath, I meant to ask? Her, or some ad writer?"

"She and Dad. Sometimes I get an inspira—"

"Well, I just thought they showed the Powers touch. I'll bet Eastman would like to think of one, just one, of those captions. So urbane."

"I don't think Mrs. Eastman—"

"All right, then, dearie. I'll leave you to it." And Miss Brown was gone.

Marion pulled up a little chair and began to sketch. Oh, yes, Linda was doing wonders for Christaman. Also for twelve other products and Linda Powers. Her work was conceded to be ravishingly close to the real thing. Art. But not, you know, so close that people didn't like it. Chances were Linda might have a show one day, and even if the serious critics could be relied upon to grimace, the public would adore it.

"Who buys pictures?" Linda would say. "The critics?" Marion, without noticing, gave the mannequin a cool wicked little smile that enhanced the charms of the negligee.

"Why, that *looks* sort of like your sister's work," Miss Brown said, materializing at her side. She probed at the sketch with sharp eyes. "Not quite the—" She spread her hands to indicate her inability to say just what it was that Linda Powers did which her sister did not. "Only, of course, I don't think Eastman will pass that. Looks a little —sassy, or something, for *this* store. After all, dearie, we specialize in half-sizes."

Marion sighed and erased the face. "This isn't a half-size."

"But the store, you know. Our *line*."

"I know."

But after Miss Brown had once again evaporated, Marion sat staring at the floor, tapping her pencil gently on the empty face of her sketch. She could, when she tried, and often when she didn't, draw lines that resembled Linda's. But, as had been pointed out, without quite the —*éclat,* she finished for Miss Brown. It occurred to her that she should be more worried at trying to do it than at not succeeding. What's *my* line? she asked herself. That's the question. She gathered her materials, after sketching in a hurried, appropriately innocent face, and started back through the department, now quieter. The workmen, apparently, had gone for lunch. All of them? She cast a quick glance around and blushed to find her rescuer leaning against a sawhorse, watching her.

"You dropped this," he said, holding out her fountain pen.

"Oh. Oh, I'd have hated to lose that. Thanks awfully." She smiled and dropped her eyes. "I seem to be thanking you for one thing and another quite a bit."

"I like it."

As I said, she reminded herself. Cheeky. She gave him a cool nod.

"You're in the art department?" he asked.

"Yes. And you?" she added deliberately, looking at his jeans, the tool in his hand.

He waved a hand. "I'm an electrician. Get all over the store."

"Indeed," Marion said.

His smile disappeared. "My mistake," he said and turned away.

Marion, filled with shame, ran after him. "Oh, please," she called softly. "Please, I didn't mean to—I was rude. I'm sorry."

"That's all right, ma'am," he said humbly, tugging his forelock. "Just that I forgot, for the moment, my place, ma'am."

Marion laughed. "You're overdoing it. One ma'am would have been enough."

"I thought it sounded good." He tilted his head, and she was relieved to see the warmth in his eyes return. "Well," he said, after a moment. "I guess . . . I'm going to lunch."

"So am I," she told him, and looked directly inviting.

"Us working people eat out of dinner pails yonder in the back," he grinned. "Otherwise I'd be happy to—" He stopped smiling and said, "Dinner, maybe?"

Marion, abruptly shy and happy, nodded. "I'd like that."

That evening Linda came into her room and said, *"Darling,* there's the most insanely handsome man down there waiting for you, where in the name of heaven did you *find* him, has he been out of the country for years, or *what?"*

"Why?"

"Well, I *mean,* we introduced each other and he'd never even heard of us, of Dad and me. You could *tell* he hadn't. That is," she added modestly, "I can understand his not having heard of me, but who, good heavens, has never heard of Dad?"

"I guess maybe lots of people," Marion said a little uncomfortably.

"He has the most *superb* Renaissance look," Linda went on, "and who *is* he?"

"John MacIntyre."

"That's been established, love. But *who?*"

"An electrician." Linda looked so completely blank that Marion repeated, "An electrician. From the store."

"Are you serious?" Linda said at last.

"Don't be a snob."

"I'm not being a snob. I'm trying to understand. What will you say to him?"

"No doubt something will occur to me."

Linda was genuinely bewildered. She even seemed to think Marion was being a little ill-bred. "I admit he's extraordinary-looking, but, after all, you're not so desperate that you have to go around picking up electricians."

"You're crude," Marion said, blinking against sudden tears.

Linda moved quickly across the room and put her arms around her sister. "Darling *child*," she murmured. "It isn't just you I'm thinking of. It's the young Adonis down there. Is it fair to him? He's obviously smitten with the house, and you're a lovely girl, and probably he'll be hurt, don't you see?"

"No, I don't," Marion said stiffening. "And you're a bit hasty."

"I don't think so," Linda said soberly. "You know I'm

right, angel. Now, go out with the young man tonight, but do, for all our sakes, put an end to it there. I just think it would be a pity for such an elegant young man to have his heart broken."

Marion pulled away from her sister's embrace. "For heaven's sake, Linda," she said wearily. "You don't even sound real."

Still, during the weeks that followed, she tried to meet Johnny away from the house, or meet him only when Linda and her father were out. Dad, in his large and casual way, had accepted Johnny, but contrived to look astonished at each re-encounter. Marion found this even more humiliating than Linda's courteous remoteness. And Johnny? He was obviously not smitten by the house, talked easily to her father when he was there and never mentioned her family when they were out together. It still left them a lot to talk about, though perhaps Linda would have been scornful. "It may be words," Marion could hear her say, "but I'd scarcely call it conversation." Yet it was such real conversation. Compliments and wonder, tales of childhood, and dreams.

"Someday I'm going to live in the suburbs," Johnny told her. His grin kept the statement impersonal. "Not very fashionable to like the suburbs, I suppose, but that's for me. Might even start a little business of my own."

Marion asked intelligent questions in an unhappy voice. Johnny, though he kept calling, kept asking for yet another date, never indicated in any way that she was particularly important, except as a nice companion. He took her to places she'd heard of but never been to. Coney Island, the Yankee Stadium, Radio City Music Hall. Sometimes they simply walked together in the park, or rode the ferry. Things, as Marion said once, that people in books did.

"People in life, too," Johnny said with amusement. Always he was sweet and warm and exciting, and never, though he kissed her as a man in love would kiss, did he say one committal word. Marion took to crying into her pillow at night. Whatever Johnny felt, she was in love, finally, completely, and she had moments of envisioning a future in which Johnny would have removed himself from the sophistication of the brownstone house, having found a girl to live with him in the suburbs. *I'm* not sophisticated, she thought. I'm no more sophisticated than . . . than a freckle. Johnny, she told him with her heart, her eyes, with everything in her voice, Johnny, I love you, please, please ask me to live in the suburbs with you. But he didn't seem to hear.

"Lamb," Linda said one day, "you'll really have to tell those store people you're leaving. We have precisely two weeks to get ready."

"Get ready?"

"Italy, Italy," Linda said sharply. "Really, I sometimes wonder who you are. A changeling? Where's my sister?"

"Where indeed?" Marion murmured. "Linda, I'm not going to Italy."

Linda didn't answer immediately. She looked at her oval magenta nails, at the Kerman rug, at the sun sifting gently through the blinds. Finally she sighed. "I suppose it's John MacIntyre?"

Marion nodded bleakly. "Not that he cares. But I—" She broke off.

"You're in love with him?"

Marion nodded.

"What do you mean, 'not that he cares'?"

"He's certainly never said anything to make me think he does."

"What does he *do?*"

"Oh . . ." Marion smiled. "From what he does, I'd say yes. Only I can't be sure, can I, if he never says so?"

"I knew he was a fool," Linda muttered.

Marion said nothing. Linda was being Linda. Hurt because Marion wouldn't take the trip, angry that Marion should be hurt, furious that the hurt should come from John MacIntyre. And she made a last attempt. "Since he doesn't say anything, wouldn't it be a good idea to come along with me?" She did not say, but conveyed the impression that an extended trip would bring Marion's emotions back into focus.

"I can't," Marion said in a low voice. No matter what that a part of their lives was past now, that there was still available.

The two sisters looked at each other wistfully, knowing that a part of their lives was past, now that there was someone more important to Marion than Linda.

Two weeks later Linda sailed alone for Italy.

"You know," Johnny said one evening, "you're different lately."

"How am I different?"

"Oh . . ." he frowned. "You don't say *indeed,* for one thing."

Marion laughed. "That does change a person so."

"And you don't blush and try to get between me and your father whenever we meet."

"Johnny, that's not fair. I never did."

"Oh, yes," he said calmly. "I knew you were afraid I'd put my foot in it somehow."

"No."

"Yes."

They were walking at dusk along Fifth Avenue. Near the Museum, Johnny halted, putting a hand on her arm. "Marion?" he said. "Honey, I *love* you."

"Oh, Johnny, Johnny, I did think you never would say it." She looked at him with brilliant eyes. "Can we live in the suburbs?"

"Wait a minute," he laughed. "I like to do my own proposing."

"I don't care who does it, just so it gets done."

"Very well, then," Johnny said. "I accept."

"Only why?" she asked him later, sitting in the library of her father's house. "Why now, and not before?"

"I'm not sure," he said carefully. "Well, yes. I suppose it's because I feel . . . a little outclassed with Linda. Until lately I wasn't so sure you didn't think so too."

She put her hand across his lips. "Darling, don't. Don't ever think such a thing."

"Like I said, Marion, you've changed. Before, I was never sure who you were. You had a way of suddenly sounding like your sister, just when I'd think I really knew you."

She shook her head. "Don't," she said again. It was a thin shadow, but she feared it might never go away.

Today, months later, married and in the suburbs, familiar with the Launderette, learning about gardens, Marion knew the shadow hadn't lifted yet. Just the sound of her sister's voice had stirred the old feelings, the long-ago wishes.

The cutlet sputtered in the pan, and she set the table, but her attention was not on these. She thought of Quebec, of being again with Linda and Dad, of talking their sort of talk, just for a little while. She loved Johnny more than anything else in the world, but maybe, just for a week—

He wouldn't want her away on her birthday, but on the other hand—

Indecisive, nervous, she stood frowning about the room for a long moment, and then abruptly gave her sister's little shrug, said in her sister's clear tone, "Oh, this is preposterous."

Of course she'd go with Linda. It was too bad that her birthday was now, but Johnny wasn't unreasonable. Even Linda knew that. And he wasn't selfish. She felt bright again, excited, now that the decision had been made, and she flew about making doubly sure that tonight the dinner would be delicious. Mushroom sauce on the cutlet. Salad with garlicked breadcrumbs. The floating-meringue pie. She decided to put candles on the table. And flowers.

Taking a pair of shears, she went out again to the garden, still light in the waning spring evening, and cut a little cluster of lilies-of-the-valley. Their odor was sweetly fragrant, and as she bent to sniff them, the robin came bobbing back toward her cellar window. She watched him curiously. He *couldn't,* she thought. Not again.

But he could.

He halted with astonishment as he spied the figure in glass, and once more made assault. This time Marion started forward before he could do himself too much damage, and he flew away.

But he'll come back, she thought. The silly thing will be going by the window again sometime and mistake an image for the real thing. One of these times he'll lay himself out just as a cat comes by.

She walked into the house thoughtfully, put the flowers in a pale blue bowl, placed them in the center of the table. Then she wheeled and went down the cellar stairs. With a damp rag and a bit of cleaner, she clouded the recently washed window.

There, she thought, that'll fix him. It was going to look odd, her one clouded window with all the others sparkling clean. But obviously the robin couldn't help himself. Someone had to.

Johnny came in as she reached the kitchen again, and she went into his arms without a word.

"Say," he asked, when he'd kissed her and held her tightly, "what's this? Is something wrong?"

"Just because I want to be kissed?"

"Because you flew at me like a bird."

Marion laughed. "I'll tell you about the bird at dinner." And in the morning she'd phone Linda. She looked at her husband lovingly, serenely. I'm not somebody's image, she thought. I'm Johnny's wife. After all, you couldn't teach a robin not to knock himself out over a reflection, but a woman could learn.

The Flirt

*I*n the living room of the sorority house, two girls occupied enormous chintz chairs and ignored each other, as people will who have accidentally been thrust together and are unsure how to separate. Carla Boyle had come in, with four volumes of modern poetry and a notebook, looking for a quiet place to explore Dylan Thomas, and had settled in the chair before becoming aware of Joan, snugly contained in another.

She'd cuddle on anything, Carla had thought, annoyed with herself for not having the courage simply to get up and leave immediately. Or on anyone, she added, silently peevish. Joan, twisting the end of a thick blond pigtail, had leaned around curiously to see who it was. Her eyes skimmed over the other girl's thin, intense face.

"Oh. Hi, Carla," she'd said. "How're you?" Impelled, always, to speak. Even to people she didn't care for and who, after all, obviously didn't care for her. "Studying?"

"Trying to."

"Oh."

Joan sank back in her chair, so that nothing but the blond top of her head was visible to Carla. She had no book and, in fact, had been just lazing in the chair,

wondering whether to go up to her room and study something, or wander across the campus to the chemist's for
a Coke and the chance of someone interesting to talk to.

Sunday, of course, was a bad day for that. Anybody interesting already had a date on Sunday afternoon, so
there would either be couples or leftovers hanging around
the chemist's. Joan didn't especially care to be seen alone
by either. Not in my weakened condition, she decided
gravely. This was the first day she'd been up in nearly a
week, which meant she'd missed a lot of classes *and* dates
having a bad cold.

She was uncomfortably aware of Carla turning pages.
She's irritated, finding me here, Joan thought. Nobody
reads poetry that fast if she's really paying attention. Joan's
course in English Literature stopped at the twentieth
century, so she'd read no modern poetry at all. Swin-
burne's sort of nice, she decided now. Not nice enough
to read when you didn't have to. But okay to study. She
sighed a little, wondering why neither of them had the
gumption to take off. We're being civilized, she thought.
Only how pointless it was when neither she nor Carla was
deceived.

For nearly four years—they were seniors now—they'd
lived together in this house, and from the first they'd had
nothing in common but distrust of each other. Carla, thin,
untidy, overanxious, passionately fond of poetry. Joan,
full-figured, casual, beautifully groomed, an indifferent
student. From the first they'd skirted each other warily,
antagonists who never admitted their hostility. In fact,

Joan thought now, probably no other girl in the house was aware of it.

Carla, turning unseen pages, wondered, why do we conceal this so carefully? Why do we continue to be courteous, to speak as though either of us cared what the other thought or felt? We're being cowardly, she thought. Children are not afraid to hate each other. But we aren't children any more. Adults would simply avoid each other. But we're not adults. We're trapped in a phase where no one dares to make the first move, for fear of looking a fool. She leafed rapidly through the book to "Fern Hill." It had never failed before to absorb her mind and heart completely. But now, reaching it, she didn't read. If Joan's mere presence could take the power of this poetry away, she didn't want to know. Because then she might really begin to hate. I don't want to hate anyone, she thought. I won't let her give me over to that sort of degradation.

Outside the window, spring lay over the campus in a veil of green-yellow. Somewhere a thrush was singing. His song came through the window screen with the sunlight and the fragrance of young leaves and flowers.

"It's a mating song," Joan said abruptly.

"What is?"

"That thrush is calling his mate."

You should know, Carla thought. A little pulse beat in her throat, but she answered carelessly, "Oh, well, I hope she shows."

"She will. Or some reasonable facsimile. He won't care."

Know all about it, don't you? Carla thought. The male psyche. Thrush or halfback, you know what they'll do. But now, it seemed, she'd be able to leave. Amenities should be observed, not impaled. She got up, gathering the books tightly to her chest. Part of her skirt hem drooped down, unsewn.

Joan twisted around once more at the sound. "Going?" There was relief in her voice.

Carla nodded and started for the door. "Things to do upstairs."

You had to say something more, didn't you? she asked herself angrily on the stairs. Couldn't just let it go, just walk out. In her room she dropped the books on the desk, walked around aimlessly, then sat on the edge of her bed, looking over the spring campus. Gradually she coaxed her mind away from Joan, gradually relaxed. *I don't care,* she said silently, boldly. I don't care about anything. And then, because it was such a silly reassurance, she began to cry.

Joan, watching Carla go, wondered why the girl always *clutched* her books so. It made her look so sort of dedicated and ridiculous. And round-shouldered. No sense of balance, thought Joan, who considered her own rather good. A little work, a little play, no torn hems. She decided she felt strong enough to go over to the chemist's.

Seth Meyers was taking a pre-medical course, but he'd been allowed to include one "frill," as his colleagues called it. The class, called simply Modern Poetry, was a thing of beauty and relaxation to Seth. Coming to it with a good knowledge of almost every living poet, he rarely studied. But the teacher, a young Englishman, read better than anyone Seth had ever heard—including the poets themselves—and to Seth it was like having a concert included in his school work.

Generally, Seth leaned back in his chair, hands in his pockets, eyes on the floor, listening to the voice of the teacher, for the entire hour. He contributed little to the classroom discussions, and often wished that the others would contribute less. Just read, he thought, and listen.

Today he frowned a little, listening to the poem Mr. Carpenter had selected. There was something . . . He shifted a bit, trying to decide what it was about the poem that disturbed him. Something not quite . . .

Mr. Carpenter closed the book, folded his hands on it, looked around the table. He looked from face to face. "Well," he said finally.

There was a vague stir, a rustle of papers. Like Seth, several of the students were frowning slightly. Because, as Seth decided, the poem *seemed* right when read from the page. It was listening to Mr. Carpenter that brought out a—flaw. He leaned his elbows on the table, holding his head, trying to ferret out the flaw he was sure existed.

"Mr. Carpenter?"

Seth glanced up. It was the . . . the Boyle girl speaking. Undernourished, eager-looking. She was mad about poetry, Seth had decided. In just that sense. Too intense. The sort of poetry lover who wants to give to the poetry as well as receive. Seth was a passive audience. He let Eliot and Ransom and Cummings give their works to him, but never, as this girl did, tried to meet them half-way. It seemed rather presumptuous. Still, watching the way she sat up now, eyes bright, with a flush on her cheeks, he wondered if perhaps she did get more than he did. If most of the people in this room got more from poetry for giving more. The thought was a little irritating. He listened to Carla suspiciously to see if this attitude of sharing with the great would give her analytical powers.

"This poem," Carla was saying, "seems really perfectly all right when you just read it to yourself." Seth began to look at her with interest. "But it's your reading," she went on to the teacher, "that brings out something . . . something bogus in it. So I suppose you saw it yourself, I mean reading it to yourself," she added, a little flustered. Mr. Carpenter smiled and waited. "Well, of course the—falseness—is there in the poem, no matter how you read it. But it isn't always easy to recognize falseness, is it? I react," she said, turning a little pedantic through nervousness, "to something in these lines that is sentimental. The tough-soft writing, where the softness is really weakness and the toughness insensitivity. Though, as I say, the thing is so well written that without someone like you to point out the failure, we might not notice it at all."

After class, Seth stopped Carla on the steps outside the building. "That was an awfully good breakdown you made there, Miss Boyle," he told her, speaking in a detaining way that showed he was prepared to go on if she would.

Carla almost closed her eyes with pleasure and surprise. From the start of the fall term she'd dreamed of a word from Seth Meyers. He'd made Modern Poetry even richer than it had been the year before, when she'd loved it. But he had always sat there, hands in the pockets of his jacket, not contributing a thing or even looking around. When the class concluded he'd always disappeared immediately, never lingering to talk with other students, to discuss a point with Mr. Carpenter. He was more like a constant visitor than a member of the class itself.

Yet here today, when she'd really forgotten all about him in the excitement of chasing that fugitive falseness, here he stood beside her, talking as though her reply would be important. So, she thought, everything comes to her who looks the other way.

She held her books tightly against her chest and looked eagerly up into his face. "But don't you agree?" she breathed. "Don't you think Mr. Carpenter read it so we'd know?"

Seth nodded. "Sure. He's a master. But I'll tell you—" He stopped and gestured down the street. "How about running over to the chemist's for a minute? We can have a Coke and talk this out."

"Oh, yes. I'd love to."

They fell into step together. Carla with a look of high rapture on her face that Seth, concentrating on what he meant to say, didn't notice.

Seth's schedule was a busy one, and until he met Carla he'd had no time for dating. Dating Carla during the weeks that followed he didn't class as dating in the actual sense at all. She was a stimulating talker, once a period of initial shyness was got over each time, and they ranged the whole field of modern poets, had a magnificent time decimating the Georgians, disagreed with a happy violence about Keats, whom Seth loved. "Oh, you're just too rigid for a man like Keats," Seth had said at last, laughing and not observing the catch of pain that sent her glance down as he spoke.

In truth, Seth didn't notice much of anything about Carla except her opinions. That he failed to notice her bitten nails, dull hair, monotonous wardrobe was the result of not caring in the least what she looked like. With the amount of work he had at present and ahead of him, he did not take time to notice what any girl looked like. That, he could see from looking around him, led to complications of late hours, flat wallets, and even heartaches. None of these fitted into the scheme of things for Seth. So, on the rare occasions when he asked a girl out, Carla was the girl he'd ask. They went to inexpensive roadhouses, drank coffee and talked about Ezra Pound.

For Carla the weeks were enchanted. She had found in Seth everything she'd ever dreamed of in a man, and considerably more than she'd dared hope for. That such a one—intelligent, inquisitive, generous-minded—should turn to her, and her alone, for she knew he saw no other girls, seemed a piece of breathless beauty from which she must almost surely wake up. Yet time went by, and she applied childish tests like pinching herself, and still on an evening once a week or so, Seth would appear at the sorority house and out they'd go for a few hours of heaven. She knew every piece of clothes he owned, every tie, every change of sweater. He did not own much, and she cherished him for that. She knew the gestures he would make, the inflections of his voice, the narrow hardness of his wrists and the black thickness of his hair.

She knew him, and she loved him very much.

In late April the house president announced at dinner that Carla had conjunctivitis.

"What's that?" said Joan, as another girl said, "Good Lord, just before exams. What a lousy break."

"It's inflammation, or something, of the eyes," the house president told Joan. "It means lying around with stuff on your eyes and bandages. In other words, dear, it means she can't see for several days, so she won't be able to study."

"That *is* tough," Joan said sincerely. She was just beginning to think about studying hard herself. Joan made a point of doing well in her work, if for no other reason than to avoid fusses with her parents or this particular house president, who was proud of the sorority's reputation for having girls who knew more than Human Relations.

Since that day when they'd sat in stiff silence together, wondering how to separate, Carla had, in some unaccountable way, altered. She was less aloof, less thin-skinned. If it had been anyone but Carla, Joan would have supposed Love. But love and Carla just didn't seem reasonable. Oh, she'd heard, from this one and that one, that Carla now had a steady date, if you could call going out for two or three hours every week or so a steady date. She'd even heard that he was attractive, but, with unwitting snobbery, discounted that. Carla was a frump, and attractive men in college did not date frumps. She had never, somehow, been here herself when this mysterious stranger turned up, and Carla hadn't once asked him to a coffee dance or tea at the house.

"The point is," the house president went on, "that I'm asking for volunteers to read to Carla."

"For how long?" a redhead down the table asked in horror.

"For as long as you're willing," the president said coldly. "I wouldn't have expected you to offer anyway." She turned to the others. "It's in ways like this we can help each other out. And, incidentally, show people the sort of sorority we have here."

"Ah," said Joan.

"What do you mean, ah?"

"Nothing special. Just . . . just that *Ah* will volunteer to read," Joan giggled.

"You will?"

"Well, sure. Why so shocked? I'm not an unkind person."

"No," the president admitted, not quite sure why she should be perplexed at the idea of Joan reading to Carla.

"I'll read for her poetry course," Joan said. "That should be easiest."

The president nodded as though things were now more normal. "Well, it's . . . nice of you to offer at all."

A few others volunteered and the topic was shelved for the remainder of the meal.

In the evening Joan knocked cautiously at the door of Carla's room. "You asleep?" she whispered.

In the room that had begun to yield to evening, Carla lay on her bed. She wore a faded dressing gown, pinned of course, Joan noticed, where a hook and eye should be. One thin arm was flung across her face, across the bandaged eye.

"No. I'm not asleep. Who's that?"

"Joan." She lifted her voice to normal. Carla made no reply at all, so she added, "I've come to read to you. We're all going to. Didn't they tell you?"

"Yes. Only not that . . . I mean, it's nice of you," Carla said remotely.

Joan, determined to be kind if it killed both of them, said, "I'll read poetry for a while, all right? And then Ann is going to do history."

Carla sighed. Her eyes hurt, and it was certainly true that for a few days she'd be unable to read, but that didn't seem a reason for their officious house president to organize any such scheme as this. Helpless and, unless she wished to be rude, at the mercy of everyone's voice. At the mercy of this voice in particular.

Why was it that she and Joan seemed destined to be

put in rooms together at times when neither of them knew how to extricate herself? She did not, since Seth, feel so strongly about Joan any more. She felt strongly about no one but Seth. Still, did that mean Joan had to get sentimental—hypocritical—and for some whimsy of her own come up here to read poetry? I don't want her to read to me, Carla thought.

She said, "Well, thanks. If you want to read some of the Hart Crane . . ." As if it's going to do me any good, she thought. How am I to be helped by a few scatterbrained girls reading for a few hours? But she wasn't going to let Joan read anything she herself liked. Let her struggle with "The Bridge," she thought, beginning to be amused. Let her try to understand that.

Joan turned on a lamp near the window. "Will this bother you?" she asked.

"No," Carla said fretfully, wishing she'd get on with it.

The evening shadows sifted into the room as Joan, in her low unaccented voice, read to her antagonist:

> " 'Series on series, infinite,—till eyes
> Starved wide on blackened tides, accrete-enclose
> This turning rondure whole, this crescent ring
> Sun-cursed and zoned with modulated fire.' "

"Magnificent, isn't it?" Carla interrupted.

"I guess so," Joan said doubtfully. "I mean, what does it mean?"

"It's Columbus' voyage to America. The voyage of discovery."

"Oh, I know. I guess I know, that is. It says so, at the top. I just don't see what these particular words mean."

There was a relaxation between them. It had come subtly, as Joan, not understanding, read on because she'd offered to. Carla turned a little on the bed, to try to tell what the blazing words might mean, and became aware of a page turning, though the voice had stopped. "What are you doing?" she asked.

"I just noticed a book here. . . . I mean, it was open, and the poem is so nice. I started reading it."

"What poem?"

"It's—let's see—'Fern Hill.' "

Carla stiffened. To explain Hart Crane was one thing. She didn't want Joan to read, to even know "Fern Hill." She tried to think of some way to prevent that low smug voice from speaking the words. But it was too late. Joan moved relentlessly into the poem, and Carla sank back, trying not to hear.

"It's pretty," Joan said, finishing.

Pretty! You idiot, Carla thought. And then, to her horror, heard Joan begin to reread lines here and there through the whole. I could scream at her to stop, Carla thought. But I'll never stop her any other way. She lay miserably for another half hour as Joan explored, apparently with pleasure, Carla's Dylan Thomas. Carla's and Seth's. But at last it was over. Joan closed the book, and Carla recognized the sounds of her rising, knew the indecisive leave-taking, and was finally alone. Or, not really.

The Flirt

For in a little while Ann, the history reader, presented herself.

"That's a good girl," said the house president, passing Joan on the stairs.

"I enjoyed it," Joan answered. "Only . . . look, I'm not sure she really likes this idea, you know. Perhaps we shouldn't . . ."

"Forget it. We're helping, aren't we?" The president continued virtuously upward. Joan, looking after her, shrugged. She'd noticed that the president hadn't offered anything in the way of volunteer reading. But the sorority was helping. *That* sort of house, said Joan to herself, and then ran downstairs as the front bell rang.

The boy at the door was tall and lean in a good hard way and his hair was black. Joan, opening to him, turned her head a little. How awfully nice, she decided. Who in the world could he be for?

"I . . . is Carla around? Carla Boyle?" he said.

Joan looked at him with astonishment. It just wasn't possible. *This* and Carla? There must be something wrong with him, she thought. She couldn't see what it could be.

"I'm Seth Meyers," he said. "Could you call her, or something?"

Joan stood back, gesturing him in. "Gosh, excuse me. I must have been dreaming. Come on in the living room. No," she added, looking over her shoulder to be sure he followed. "That is, yes, she's in. But she has conjunctivitis and is lying in a dark room listening to people read things."

Seth looked concerned. "That's bad," he said. "They've had a doctor?"

Joan nodded.

"I just had a couple of hours, so I thought I'd run over and surprise her." He looked around the room uncertainly. Several of the girls there nodded, recognizing him. Some looked shrewdly at Joan, who eyed them blandly back. She wasn't doing anything. Just explaining.

"Come on over here in the window seat," she said. "I'll explain." She patted the seat, which was in half darkness, and settled beside him. "You see, she has this eye thing, so we're all taking turns reading to her."

"Did you read?" he asked.

Joan, who had an ear for variations in the male inflection, caught the shift of his interest from whether Carla was being read to, to whether Joan had read. She felt the warm rise of pleasure that a man's awakened interest gave her. An instinctive warmth, one that she could trust.

She nodded slowly. "Where did you meet Carla?" she asked with a directness that seemed to indicate interest in Seth only as he was connected with Carla.

Unreasonably, he resented that. "We take Modern Poetry together. It's a marvelous class," he said, wondering why he sounded so defensive. Probably—he attempted detachment—probably because this girl with the beautiful figure and the shining hair summoned to his mind pictures of dances and football games. The things he didn't have time for. The girls he didn't have time for. He wondered, suddenly, why Carla's hair always seemed so lank. Vitamin deficiency, maybe. Or not enough fresh air.

"What're you reading to her?" he said, keeping the conversation to Carla, as though he sensed danger. Late hours, flat wallets, even heartaches. Not for Seth Meyers.

"Poetry," Joan said, watching him closely. "Hart Crane. And . . ." She broke off dreamily.

"What are you thinking?" he asked after a moment's brimming silence.

Joan looked up a little, into his eyes. "I was thinking of those lines from 'Fern Hill' . . . *'Before the children green and golden, Follow him out of grace . . .'* "

She hesitated. Actually, they were the only two lines in the poem she could recall. But she *had* liked them, so it wasn't dishonest to seem to know more than she quoted. She would know more, because she planned to read lots of modern poetry now. There were—she glanced at Seth and away—all sorts of reasons for reading poetry. It would really be narrow not to try the moderns.

"He's a wonder, isn't he?" Seth said, referring to Dylan Thomas. He laughed a little. "Funny, isn't it, the different people who like poetry? I mean, I'd have said, looking at you, 'now, there's a girl made for dancing and chrysanthemums.' You know."

Joan's voice was ripe with delight. Oh, she loved this part . . . this first awareness of coming conquest. "You think that everyone has to be . . . Oh, that you can't care what your clothes look like, and still like poetry. Is that it?"

Seth looked at her soft white sweater, her trim flannel skirt, her bright hair. "I don't know what I thought," he answered, bemused. He sighed, and then snapped his fingers. "Look, I've got an idea—"

"I hoped you might have," she said softly.

The medical student who hadn't had time for girls now hadn't time to defend himself. The battle was engaged before he'd even prepared to fight. He asked Joan to go out.

"When?"

"Well, now, of course."

"But you said you only had a couple of hours. Seems hardly worth while to start at that rate."

Seth shook his head. "I don't have to get back, really. There's nothing I couldn't take care of tomorrow."

Joan smiled and rose. "I'll get a jacket." She stood fragrantly close to him for a second. "In a minute . . . Seth."

As she passed Carla's door, upstairs, she could hear Ann struggling with the defections of Charles I. She hesitated, standing in the hall, the sweater trailing. After all, in college, or in life, girls like Carla would always lose out. If she didn't lose Seth to Joan, most surely she would to someone else. Girls, smart ones, wouldn't leave him indefinitely to talk poetry with Carla. And I saw him first, she thought. Or, anyway, first after Carla. Why doesn't she wake up? Joan thought angrily. What does she expect, trailing around in safety pins and soiled skirts?

She put the sweater on and walked to the stairs. Besides, she thought, I don't care much for Carla, and Carla definitely doesn't like me. Why should I do her any favors?

Going down, she realized one thing further. At the moment she didn't much like Carla, but she didn't like herself any better. That was a sickening admission. Again she paused, hand on the railing, hoping that somehow, without volition, she'd turn and go back upstairs. Send someone down with an excuse. It wouldn't hurt her, or Seth either. They meant nothing to each other. He and Carla did. She could imagine what Seth might mean to Carla.

But then the Joan who flirted, who believed it was every girl for herself, suddenly shrugged. She didn't like herself. Well—that would happen now and then. She thought it must happen to everyone. She wasn't going to let it bother her.

Not with Seth waiting at the bottom of the stairs, waiting to be won.

The Wedding
and The Wonder

*B*eneath the dock, under the warm old sun-dried boards on which they sat, Peg and Vince could hear the changeling waters swirl and sigh. Out there the lake was broad and calm, ruffled by boat or swimmer, but under its glinting surface very deep. Here, under the jetty's ancient bones, shallow waters were all exuberance, all slipping and whispering around slim piles. Peg tried to see through a crack. She knew how it was under there. Shadowy, a little cool, with bars of dusty sunlight drifting in the hollow place between the water and the slick dark boards. And, if you spoke, a thin vibrant echo.

She smiled and turned her head toward Vince, who was watching Chris Donaldson cut across the lake on his new water skis. Vince's black curls glistened wetly, drops of water were drying slowly on his tawny skin, and he squinted, watching the speedboat cavort, the superb Chris sail in its wake.

"I can see it," Peg said lazily.

"See what?"

"The pain that Chris is giving you in your neck," she told him.

He swiveled to see her. "Nothing a couple of aspirins and a drowning won't cure."

"You're making it very hard for people, you know." Peg spoke idly, as though what she said was not important and might have been something else altogether—a comment on the weather, a suggestion that they eat ice cream. "After all, Ginny *is* your sister, and I should think you'd —oh, act so she'd feel good."

"She feels fine. What the heck—do you think anything I think matters?"

Peg wriggled her toes and shoulders. "I think I'll be a sun worshiper," she said.

"What do you mean, you'll be?"

"Oh, you know. Sacrifice something. I'll burn my piggy bank on the altar of the sun at midnight."

"Just like you," Vince said. "Make a sacrifice to the sun in the middle of the night."

He was smiling now, but Peg was not heartened. In a moment, unless they left the dock altogether and walked up to their houses, he'd be back on the subject of Chris Donaldson and woe, woe to life as they had known it. "Here he comes," Vince would say, had said many times, "looking like the spirit of the Acropolis, flapping his brains at everybody so we can feel how good the gods are, turning the whole place upside down." He'd trail off, scowling, and Peg would go on wondering what to answer, except that she thought Chris was pretty nice, and obviously she couldn't say that.

"I'm going home," she said. "I'm hungry."

"I suppose we might as well."

As they got to their feet, the boat's motor was cut, and in the sudden silence they watched Chris detach himself from the skis and clamber aboard. Ginny moved over and he took the wheel. The motor sprang to life again and the boat nosed into its little shed near the jetty.

"Hey, wait for us," Ginny called. "We know it's lunchtime." She ran toward them, spray-wet and laughing, with Chris at her side. *"Did* you see Chris on the skis? Isn't he marvelous? Vinny, why don't you try it? I'll drive ever so carefully, and if you fall off I'll speed right back for you."

Vince set his jaw. "I'm not afraid of them, Ginny, if that's what you mean. I can ride the old water skis as good as—I can ride them perfectly well, if I want to."

"Sure he can," Chris said. "There's no trick to it, really. Just balance."

Vince elected to take this as a slur, and marched off in silence.

"Oh, what *is* the matter with him?" Ginny said in a puzzled way. "Peg, do you think he's got growing pains? He's so *cross* lately."

Peg looked at Vince's pretty older sister, thinking, She really doesn't know. Isn't it funny, because Ginny's not stupid, and she's usually very good at feeling out Vince's troubles. But then, that was the whole bother now. Ginny was too in love, too absorbed with love, with

Chris, with her wedding in less than a week, to have the old sensitivity to other people, to Vince especially. Ginny was—what? Twenty-two. Six years older than Vince, and practically his mother since their own had died. But not really, because a mother doesn't just forget what a boy feels, and a sister in love apparently does.

Peg shook her head. "I don't know, Ginny. Just a mood, I guess."

"But you two are always together. Doesn't he say anything? *Wouldn't* you think he'd be happy and pleased, now of all times?" Ginny pleaded.

"Oh, he'll come around," Chris said. That was what they all said lately, as though Vince were a late bus or a delayed meal, something held up but fundamentally predictable.

Honestly, Peg thought, some people are so thick. She shook her head again and turned toward her own house. "See you later," she said, and walked quickly across the road that separated the big houses like Vince's father's from smaller ones like her own parents'. She went between the privet hedges, along the flagged walk to the screened kitchen door. "Hi, Mom," she said. "Oh, good, lobster salad." She started to sit down.

"You'll stick to that chair," her mother said. "You're wet. Vincent still sulking?"

"I suppose so." That's not what I mean, really not, Vince. I mean that you're hurt, that you're sad. But we mustn't give you away. Suddenly she felt tears, stinging and surprising. Poor Vince. She turned away, rubbing her eyes, but her mother didn't seem to notice and the tears subsided. She picked up a piece of celery, cool, damp, crisply ridged, and rubbed it along her cheek. She bit into it. "You know, Mom, it's a very peculiar thing how apparently people have only room for one emotion at a time. You'd think just because a person was in love they wouldn't have to forget everyone around them and how they were feeling, wouldn't you?"

Her mother sorted out this sentence, pulled the bowl of lobster away from Peg and let her hands fall to her lap. "Perhaps. Love reacts . . . differently on different people. Ginny's never been in love before, and she's been taking care of Vince and their father for years. I suppose now she feels that this time of her life should be all her own, and that people should understand."

"I suppose you think Vince is being selfish."

"I don't know what he's being. I guess he's hurt, and upset. He's too young to disguise his emotions. And, then, Ginny's never made him feel he had to. Perhaps it was a mistake for her to give him so much of her time, so much understanding . . . if she couldn't keep it up. But how can people tell ahead? It's terribly hard, darling. Really, terribly hard."

"She hasn't been taking care of them altogether, you know. They have a couple, which is more than most of us have."

"You know quite well what I mean. Anyway, you have a couple too. Me and your father."

Peg laughed. But as she went upstairs the smile slid

away, and there she could see Vince again, looking over the water with his unhappy eyes. Well, her mother had guessed, but she'd expected that. Ginny, it seemed, either hadn't, or refused to do anything about it if she had.

She took off her bathing suit, put on a cotton bathrobe and sat at her dressing table, on which there were one jar of cold cream and one lipstick. She patted the cream on her face, making lacy ridges and sworls, getting some of it on her thick chestnut hair. Outside, the cicadas' long reed song filled the hot noon air. The trees at her window might have been painted there, and no bird moved in the still branches. In the house the kitchen radio played low music and the flat clink of silver sounded as her mother set the table.

During the week it seemed as though the house waited, delicately poised, for her father's return. Then, with his heavy tread and voice, with the radio suddenly loud, with the laughter and all the talking, and people coming in and going out, the house settled down comfortably. Ah, it seemed to say, I knew there was something missing. Well, thought Peg, removing cold cream with dreamy indifference, I suppose Ginny is looking forward to something like that. Marriage and a house fulfilled.

Certainly Mr. Edwards, who, like her own father, commuted on weekends during the summer to this lake colony, couldn't make a house behave practically like a dog, waiting for him. Ginny could try her best, but to Mr. Edwards the house by the lake was just something he had to take a train to get to, and thank heaven for Labor Day when they could sensibly move into the city again. Vince and Ginny adored the lake house and their summers here. (How long had they all been coming? Oh, years. Peg was fifteen now, and she could remember playing with a bucket, wearing a tiny pair of shorts, and *that* was a long time ago.) But Mr. Edwards went on being the man from the city. He strolled by the lake in his flannels and never went swimming. He bought the speedboat, but never went out in it. He brightened only toward the end of August, when everyone else began to look lonely and wistful.

"Peg!" her mother called. "I thought you wanted this lobster salad."

Peg jumped. "O.K. I just have to duck into the shower." She ran down the hall in her bare feet, giving her thoughts of Mr. Edwards a final courteous shove. He was the sort of man who did his best by his children, only his best was the kind that was charged and sent from the finest stores, not handmade or carried home in a friendly bundle.

Poor Vince, she thought. Poor darling. She wondered, suddenly, where Ginny planned to go after she was married. The thought was an icicle. If Ginny and her gorgeous Chris didn't want to come to the lake? If they went somewhere else, to be alone together, even after their honeymoon? But then Mr. Edwards might very well sell the house. Would he keep it just for Vince? Would doing his best include that? The shower sprang at her, and these frightening thoughts.

And as she skimmed downstairs, she was promising

Vince to understand now. Not to scold him any more for being morose. After all, she was on his side. Ginny was lovely, and weddings divine. But Vince was Vince, and he was more important.

The wedding was to take place at four o'clock on Friday afternoon in the little white wooden church they'd attended on summer Sundays for years. Mr. Edwards, who'd thought surely the city, the large church on the Avenue, was at first annoyed, then dryly resigned. "If I must give you away," he said in his maturer-element-of-the-Yale-Club voice, "then the site of the sacrifice is of secondary importance. We must make you happy, dear."

Yes, we must bear that in mind, Peg thought, listening to this conversation that was taking place once again. Mr. Edwards had been giving in gracefully for weeks, and now, with the wedding only five days away and settled to the last detail, was doing it again. Ginny, curled on the sofa next to Chris, smiled at her father to show how much she appreciated his thoughtfulness. Chris rubbed his chin and grinned. It was going to take more than Mr. Edwards to throw him off stride. More than Vince, too, Peg thought, watching Ginny's brother sitting in a silent slump in an easy chair near the door.

It was late Sunday afternoon, and they were all waiting for a little more time to pass so that Mr. Edwards could leave for his train.

"You're going tonight, sir?" Chris had inquired. He "sirred" Mr. Edwards firmly, and Mr. Edwards seemed not to mind.

"Yes, I'll have to be in the office early tomorrow. You could ride in with me, of course," he'd added uninvitingly.

"Well, thank you, that's a good thought, sir. But I'll just stay around with Ginny. Take her out to dinner or something. I'll go in later."

"Fine, fine," Mr. Edwards had said, making the rest of them smile.

"It's a nice day," Chris said after a while.

"Beautiful," Ginny agreed.

Everyone looked out the French windows. Yes, very beautiful.

A clock ticked. Mr. Edwards stretched out his legs, drew them back so that his feet were planted under him in the right position for getting up presently.

Ginny looked at her brother, glanced up at Chris, who gave her a small wink. But how awful it is, Peg thought, that no one is helping their happiness. They're holding it all alone, and no one smiles on it and says, "How nice, isn't it lovely, we're glad for you." They must know. They were like a young couple holding a new baby, loving it, happy in it, but surely aware that everyone turned away, and that was not how it should be.

"Ginny," Peg said in a bright warm voice, "do you realize how close it is? Aren't you just simply dying of happiness? I mean, I can hardly wait to see your dress and veil. Can I come over while Mrs. Roder presses it? I could hold the hem or something, couldn't I?" She wouldn't, she would *not* look at Vince. She smiled gaily at Ginny, who responded with delicate pleasure to a chance of discussing her wedding dress.

Chris gave Ginny a look of devotion, as Ginny said, "On Friday morning, you know. We'll press it early in the morning, and the veil will have to be pressed too."

On the lawn fat robins bounded. A jay walked around the stone birdbath, drinking, but disdaining to wash up. In the room words were spoken of the wedding. Peg laughed and agreed and thought Maine was *wonderful* for a honeymoon, and where in Maine did they—

"Chris has a little house in Bar Harbor, so we—"

"Well, not really *in,* dear," Chris said. "You see, it's sort of outside on an old road."

"And if we like it," Ginny hurried on, oblivious of all but the happiness that was hers now for the taking, "we may just go up there summers all the time."

Vince stood up. "I've got some things to do." He turned, but his father said:

"I'll be leaving directly myself. Aren't you going to drive me to the train?"

"Oh. Oh, sure, Dad. Sure." He stood beside his chair, looking out at the birdbath. The jay was gone, the water in the stone curve unruffled.

"Well—" Mr. Edwards cleared his throat—"I'll be getting on. Heavy week ahead, and I'll have to get out here early on Friday, of course."

"Friday?" Ginny said. "But the rehearsal is Thursday night. You have to give me away." She sounded desperate at this threat to perfection in her wedding. "Everything has to be exactly right, Dad," she cried. "It really does."

"I'm sorry, my dear, but it's quite impossible. I have a very important client coming in from Cleveland Thursday evening. And, after all—" he laughed a little—"after all, important clients help foot the bills for important daughters."

He stood up, buttoning his jacket, giving the impression of a man delighted to leave but attempting to seem reluctant. He was not successful and his jaunty step going down the walk betrayed him, if his voice had not. Ginny looked after him with expressionless eyes.

Peg, as Vince got into the car and reached for the starter, suddenly ran through one of the French doors. "May I ride along?" she shouted.

Mr. Edwards winced at the gusto of her voice, but he edged over to let her in beside him, and they started for the station. The drive was short and the train, to everyone's relief, on time. Vince swung quickly out of the station plaza as his father left them.

"You want to go right back?" he asked.

"No, Vince. Not if you don't."

"Let's ride a little."

"All right. You can have dinner with us," she added. Mrs. Roder would fix him something if Chris took Ginny out. But Vince shouldn't be alone this week. He was too aware of how alone he'd be when it was over.

He nodded and smiled at her, turned back to the road. It was evening now, but there was no breath of dark in the air. The birds, quiet all afternoon, sang in hedges and trees, darted over the fields on either side of them. On the rim of a meadow, against the sky, a herd of lowing cows swayed home. One of them wore a bell that sounded a wooden sweet note in the high evening air. Vince drove slowly and, without asking, turned down a small lane that led to the lake's edge. Low branches scraped the car's sides, and once he had to duck a higher one. In a clearing he stopped, pulling on the brake.

"Come on, Peg. Let's sit there, by the water."

So they did. They sat on the grass, watching the small waves curl at the lake's shore, tug at the long grasses that grew beneath the water. The lake and sky were lime and gold and berry red as the sun set behind them, and a canoe drifted past, far out, soundlessly.

Vince exhaled a long breath. "It's nice, isn't it? Peaceful."

"I wonder why people like the water so much."

"Because we came out of it."

"Did you read that somewhere?"

"I guess so." He smiled. "Maybe it's true. Don't you ever wonder about it, Peg? Where we've come from, where we're going? Or why? Mostly why."

"I do, sometimes. But thoughts like that—they're so overpowering. I begin to get sort of weak, and my brain pants like a dog. So it's easier just not to. I stop and hurry back to thinking about tennis or something."

"Tennis isn't anything to *think* about," Vince said peacefully. "We could play some tomorrow, if you wanted."

"Oh, sure." She picked up a twig and drew it lightly

along her leg, watching the white line appear against her tan skin.

"I suppose if they do decide to go to Maine," Vince said, taking the twig away from her, "my father'll sell the house. He'd be only too glad."

They plunged together, head first, into misery.

"I know that you think I'm being pretty awful about all this," he said quickly. "I know it, and I guess I am. But, my gosh, here comes this guy, out of nowhere, and in three months he's ruined everything I care about. Ginny and I haven't said two words except 'Chris' all summer, and now he pulls a house in Maine out of his hat and where does that leave me?"

"I suppose you could go with them," she said without pleasure.

"I don't want to go with them. I want to be here, where we've always been." He shut his eyes tight, opened them again and stared fiercely out at the water. "You're thinking that all I'm thinking about is me—but it isn't, really, Peg. I'm . . . I guess I'm missing a time of life that all of us had. Your folks, and Ginny. You and me," he added softly.

"It's been so *nice* here, and we've all been happy. I suppose you and your folks will go on being happy," he said with a sort of sad surprise. "But I don't see what's so awfully selfish about being—about not being wildly delighted over the whole thing." He tossed the twig away.

Peg looked down at her fingers winding around one another. Her throat hurt when she swallowed. All very well for Ginny to be offended, for her own mother to say Vince was sulky, for Chris and her father to predict indifferently that he'd "snap out of it." But they weren't having the nicest part of their lives tossed out. Ginny would have her new world, and Chris. Her own parents would just go on as before. But Vince—he'd have no sister, no house by the lake. He'd have Mr. Edwards and the apartment in the city. And she—she would have no Vince. Peg shivered a little.

"Want to go back?" Vince asked.

She turned to him suddenly. "Look, darling, you can come to our house in the summertime."

Vince turned his head and looked at her without speaking. Their faces were very close, their eyes motionless on each other.

"Why did you call me that?" he said then.

"Why?" she repeated softly. "Well, because—" She stopped. Why? Because that was how she thought of him. He was Vince darling. Only, until this moment she hadn't known what it meant. She had thought it meant *Vince is a darling, and I'm very fond of him*. It didn't. It meant *Vince darling, I love you*.

"Peggy," he said curiously. "Peggy, how is it we didn't know before?"

She shook her head slowly. "I don't know. All this time . . . and we never knew."

They continued to look at each other with trembling brilliant surprise at the wonder of it, and were pierced with a sort of happiness they had never dreamed of, could never have dreamed. I love you, he said without speaking. And, oh, me too, she told him silently. Me too.

"Look," he said, taking her hand, "look, Peg. Don't say anything. Don't let anyone know. Because they'd think —people just don't think that if you're under twenty you can really be in love. They think it's—it's—"

"Practice," Peg said. They smiled at each other, and at the rest of the world. "But, Vince, I wouldn't, I couldn't, I *never* would."

"I know," he said. "I know, I know. I know." He jumped up suddenly, laughing. "Come on, beautiful, let's go home and eat." He pulled her to her feet "Let's, Peg. Before," he added, in a husky voice not at all like a boy's, "before I eat you."

He let her off at the back door. "I'll see you in a bit," he said, as she stood beside the car. "I'll change for dinner and be right back." Still he didn't start the car, and she didn't move. "Peggy?"

"Yes, Vince?"

He smiled. "Just—Peggy. That's all."

After he'd gone, she walked slowly to the house, taking deep steadying breaths and hoping she wouldn't glitter so with happiness that everyone would see it on her, like a fall of bright snow.

"Oh, there you are, darling," her mother said.

"Here I am," she said unconcernedly. "O.K. if Vince comes for dinner?"

"Of course. You know, Peg," her mother went on a bit sternly. "Ginny is not very happy. Her father—oh, that *man!*—won't come back in time for the rehearsal, and the poor child is miserable. What sort of family *is* that?"

"Vince says he'll give her away in the rehearsal." ("Heck," he'd said on the way home in the car, "I'd be glad to.") "And I suppose a brother is practically as good as a father."

"Oh, isn't that *fine*," her mother was saying. "Ginny will be so pleased. Now, I *knew* that boy would come around."

Peg's father rattled his paper. "These things are never as important as they seem," he told them.

Though
I Know She Lies

*H*e came suavely down the aisle on his way to the dining car, six feet of what every college boy should be, and the girl who'd been staring out the train window for an unseeing hour turned as he passed. She caught her breath and made a slight forward motion, then sank back and followed him with her eyes as he went through the heavy door at the far end of the car.

The girl pressed her gloved hands together, and her rather lovely face stiffened as she sat remembering an unanswered letter, an unreturned telephone call.

He's horrible, she thought then. Horrible. All boys are, and all men, but Marc Jamison, with his high head and his manners—is it real manners not to answer a letter, not to reply to a telephone call?—is the absolute worst of them all.

The rain stopped, some people got on and a woman seated herself next to Katherine and began to talk. Freezing outdoors, she said it was. Colder than the top of your refrigerator. "Am I glad to be inside at last! Do you know this train is twenty minutes late already? When in the world we'll get to Boston— You going to Boston?"

"Yes."

"Back to school, is that it?"

Katherine gave her a curt nod.

Not put out, the woman rambled on about the train, about her son, about what ages it had been since *she'd* been in school.

Katherine turned her head to the window, willing the woman to stop, and then when the voice did abruptly cease, she felt abashed.

"I'm sorry," she said, hoping desperately that these words would not start another spate of talk. "I—ah—I've had a bereavement. I can't talk, sort of. It's too—" She broke off. Stupid words, silly lie. Anyone could see through them.

The woman did not seem to. Her face fell in heavy sympathy, and she gently patted Katherine's entwined fingers.

"There," she said. "There, there. I'm sorry." She fell silent; but her eyes darted about, and Katherine could see she was wishing she'd chosen any seat but this, next to a bereaved girl who didn't even want to talk about it. All the way to Boston, Katherine thought for the woman, and the girl won't talk.

A compulsive natterer, Katherine told herself. Natterer had been a favorite expression of an English teacher she had had last term. A real English teacher—from England, and just a month ago he'd gone back to England.

Katherine had been absolutely sure she loved him, and this love—secret and almost holy—had kept her from minding that she hadn't had ordinary dates like ordinary girls. She had moved, she felt, in an aura both tender and aloof. And then he was going, and she had never told anyone of her love. It was worse than that. Somehow, as soon as she knew he was leaving, she didn't *have* her love. It was like a dream in which you suddenly find yourself naked in a room full of extravagantly dressed people. Defenseless before her world, she'd wept for the young Englishman. She was no longer a girl cloaked and protected by an unnamed love, but a girl who just never had any dates and was no asset to the sorority house.

And she could imagine the comments of the other girls. "How did she get in this house, anyway?" someone would ask, and some other one would answer, "Well, she *looked* okay. How could we know she's just not with it?"

Oh, I know how they must talk, she thought. And I didn't ever really think I seemed tender and aloof. I just *wanted* to think it. How can I think something is true and know that I only wish it were true?

When my love swears that she is made of truth, I do believe her, though I know she lies. . . .

It was, to Katherine's mind, the loveliest and the saddest of the sonnets of Shakespeare. She could hear the young English instructor's voice dealing with it gently, paying out its beauties like a silken rope with which to catch the consciousness of his students.

She sighed, and the woman next to her moved restlessly

but did not speak. Katherine leaned her head back, then jerked it away from contact with the seat. "Never," her mother had said, among such admonitions, "lean your head back in a train. Heaven knows whose heads have been leaning there before you." She was also never to eat in a roadside diner, never to put a public telephone to her ear, never to accept a ride from anyone except the minister.

There were a lot of things that were either unwise or unfastidious, and some of them she remembered, some—because she had never shared all her mother's alarms—she forgot. What she could not forget was the anxiety her mother had felt whenever Katherine had a date: Did the boy drive carefully? It didn't *matter* if the other girls stayed out late, Katherine must be in by eleven. After a while it had seemed easier to accept no dates at all. And imperceptibly—she didn't know just when it had happened—she came to be that listless sort of girl that boys just don't ask for dates.

Now that she was in college, her mother wanted her to have dates. To keep her from being disappointed, to keep her from asking too many questions, Katherine made some up. Poor mother, she thought. Poor me.

Sometimes she wondered why she didn't quit the sorority and live in a dormitory, though, in truth, she knew perfectly well why she did not. She wouldn't leave if they didn't ask her to, and it was rather late in the day for that. She would not, because when she was home she could talk cozily about her house and the crazy things that went on in it, stories she told mostly to friends of her mother's. But sometimes at the beach club she met people her own age, people she'd gone to school with, and she'd join them for a while and tell untrue, happy stories and laugh a lot.

She stared at the door at the far end of the car.

A year ago she'd written Marc Jamison a letter. A bright, tossed-off note saying a couple of witty things about how she'd just broken her engagement to a young actor and now was heart-whole, but the asinine trouble was she'd been giving him so much of her time exclusively for so long that now she found herself without a date for a little sorority house party, and suddenly she'd remembered her handsome cousin was actually going to the nearby university, and so on.

He hadn't answered.

A year was a long time. Plenty of time in which to convince yourself that somehow your note had gone astray. So, this Christmas vacation she'd called his apartment in New York City. If she could manage, manage even once, to get him over to the house, he *might* want to come back.

If he did not return, she could tell everyone there'd been a desperate quarrel. "It's been . . . I don't know," she'd say, her eyes wide, infinitely sad, "a thing that I've known would happen, that I didn't want to happen. Marc is a boy who can care so terribly, and I—oh, I'm a will-o'-the-wisp." Too exaggerated? Well, she could find *something* to say.

But once, at least, she would have had a boy for a party. She would have been part of the dragonfly ritual of dressing, skimming over perfume bottles, buzzing up-stairs and downstairs, flitting past windows and mirrors. And any one of those girls would have lived on pemmican for a year to be responsible for Marc's presence. He was riveting.

He'd been out when she called, and he hadn't called back.

Suddenly Katherine got to her feet.

"Going someplace?" said the woman beside her.

"The dining car," Katherine said.

"Want me to go with you?"

"No! I mean—excuse me, please. I didn't mean to sound like that. But my cousin is in there, and I have to talk to him."

She walked down the aisle quickly, wavered halfway and stopped. I don't want to, she thought. I can't. She turned around, met the woman's steady eyes, gave a little wave as though that were what she'd intended, and faced forward again, feeling both ill and faintly, only faintly, hopeful.

Maybe he'd been too busy, really too busy, to answer her phone call. Maybe he'd tried some time when she hadn't been in.

She walked into the dining car and saw him alone at a table. He was drinking coffee and smoking, and he looked . . . she thought the word would be "urbane." Self-reliant, sure of his place in the world. I'll never bring it off, she thought. And then: *Courage, Katherine.*

She advanced, drew up sharply at his table. "Well . . .

Marc! For goodness' sake, it's Marc Jamison. How *are* you?"

"Uh-why, fine." He was on his feet, like the perfect gentleman he possibly was. "I was just finishing up, but—" He indicated the seat across from him with a gesture that even Katherine, in a mood to conquer, could only find half-hearted.

It was too late, however, for mild deterrents. "Lovely," she said, and sat down, obliging him to. "I just hate to eat alone."

She snatched up a menu and studied it so as not to meet his eyes for a crucial moment or two while he adjusted to the idea of remaining. "Why don't you have some more coffee?" she suggested, not looking up. Then the waiter was there. She ordered something, looked back to Marc and smiled deliciously. "Oh, you *are* a one. Or did you call me back and I just wasn't there? I practically never am, but I should hate to think I'd missed your call."

"Well, no. That is—I was confoundedly busy this vacation. You know how it is."

"Do I ever." She gave a half-laughing, reminiscing sigh. "All past, now. And here we are, on our way to buckle down. Look, Marc, I'm going to be outright unmaidenly and repeat an invitation I made you last year. We're having this little roundelay at my house—"

"Don't tell me you're still moping over that guy, the actor or whoever?"

So the letter hadn't been miscarried! She'd never thought it had. But she didn't want to be nonchalant about it as well as the phone call, and so let it pass. "Oh. Oh, yes. No, that's all over. As a matter of fact, he called me not too long ago—but that's neither here nor there. No, Marc," she said, leaning forward a little, looking into his eyes—her own were lovely and she knew it and she could see Marc knowing it, too, in spite of his restlessness—"I'm asking you just because I'd like to have you. Seems a good reason, doesn't it, Marc?"

He got out another cigarette, lit it, twirled the match in his fingers, dropped it in the ashtray, watched for a moment while she buttered a roll, and said, "Well, gosh. That's nice of you, Katherine. Uh—very nice of you."

Ah, thought Katherine, and knew that she had her man. Or, at any rate, had him pigeonholed. With a little more effort, she might very well be the victor in this skirmish. Marc Jamison, gentleman, college sophomore, cousin something-or-other-removed, was the type who could drop a letter unanswered in his wastebasket and ignore a phone message, but face to face with somebody—*anybody*, probably—didn't know how to say no. In other words, Katherine thought with understanding, a moral coward. She pressed on, and by the time her coffee was brought, Marc had agreed to be her guest at the dinner dance in early March.

He offered to pay for her lunch, and she refused. He did not suggest that they ride the rest of the way to Boston together, as she had hoped he would. But, going back to her seat, she found it difficult to look properly bereft for her traveling companion, and gradually they began talking.

Katherine mentioned the town from which she came and then the names of a famous author, a famous actor, a famous scientist, all of whom lived there. Her manner of mentioning their names was most respectful and intimate. "But then I've lived in the town my whole life," she said modestly, "so naturally I'd know everybody."

She explained that her studies would lead eventually to a law degree and that the following summer she was going to travel in Europe on her own.

"All by yourself?" the woman said, rather coolly. "Won't you be afraid?"

"Oh, heavens, no," said Katherine. "I'm always doing things alone." This unadorned, inadvertent truth alarmed her, and she hurried to dress it up. "I mean, I *need* to be alone sometimes. After all, you spend the whole year surrounded by people and there comes a time when it simply won't do. Don't you ever feel that way?"

The woman said she supposed so, sometimes.

As the train pulled into the station, they gathered their things, and the woman spoke for the last time. Katherine definitely found something acerb in her tone. "You seem to have recovered nicely. That is, you're bearing up well."

At once Katherine felt diminished, found out. "It was talking to you," she said in a flat, vague voice. "You've been such a help." She felt herself smiling with a horrible insincerity; then she fled.

Though I Know She Lies

"There is no excuse for lying," people said. Well, there might not be an excuse, but sometimes there were reasons. I have reasons, Katherine thought. The trouble was that sometimes even the reasons didn't seem like an excuse.

But none of it mattered now. Not the woman on the train or the lies that came to her tongue. Not the gray weather outside or the gray politeness they showed her at the house. Marc was coming for the dinner dance, and after they saw him they'd sing a different tune, all right. To get a boy like Marc coming back, they'd put a little color in their courtesy. They'd probably even be friendly, she thought with scorn. She didn't care for their courtesy or their friendship. I mean, she said to herself, if you can't be liked for yourself alone, the heck with it. Only just show them.

One evening, when the housemother and two or three sorority sisters were in the parlor, Katherine said, "Mrs. Corson, I'm having a guest for the dinner dance next week."

"Are you?" said Mrs. Corson. She tried to smother the surprise in her voice. "That's nice, Katherine. Who is it? Some young man you met on the holidays?"

"Goodness, no. Someone I've known for simply ages." She was darned if she'd say that Marc was her cousin, even if she removed him twenty times and cubed it. She could not, either, figure any way to ask him not to mention it. Well, just hope he wouldn't, and don't worry about it. "Ages," she repeated. "I've—it's only lately I've *felt* like doing things. Gay, dancy things, you know."

She turned away abruptly, wanting to leave just a misty impression of some loss she'd suffered.

"What's he like?" said one of the girls unexpectedly.

"Like? Like—anybody, I guess."

Given nothing at all to build on, she could throw up a structure of fancy that seemed solid to anyone who didn't actually attempt to touch it. But, given a reality—like Marc—she could think of nothing to say. How do you make a story out of the truth? Marc was coming, and he was real. There was nothing to add. Let him burst on them like a dazzling sun.

"Nothing special," she added, and thought of the specialness of Marc and how they would notice it and how, perhaps, they would recall her remark and wonder how she could not have found him special.

Two days before the dance she was called to the phone, and when she heard her name yelled up the stairway, with that "Phone call; want to take it up there?" she knew with bitter certainty that it would be Marc, that he was not coming, that he would have some stumbling story to offer that she would have to accept. That she was not, after all, going to have a date for the party. She went to the phone like Anne Boleyn to the block, self-controlled and terrified.

"Yes? Yes, hello?" she said dimly.

"Oh, Katherine. That you? Say, this is Marc. Marc Jamison."

"I recognize your dear voice," she said, playfully now.

Make it hard for him. Anyway, even if no one was directly lounging around in the hall to overhear, she was unquestionably being overheard. Make it hard for him, and don't let *them* know. Her mind flipped rapidly over possible ways of saving face. It would just have to be a disease. There was no time to think of anything else. She'd pretend he was calling to say he'd come down with something.

"Listen, Katherine," he pleaded, "I'm in a real swivet. I mean, I just plain can't get away this weekend. I thought I could, but the plain fact is I can't."

He stopped, and Katherine wondered if he planned not even to give an explanation. Just "I can't" and that was all? She decided to give him gallstones and hoped they were very painful. "Oh, what a pity!" she exclaimed. "And when did this attack—"

"Thing is," he went on, as if she hadn't spoken, "fellow I know here says he'll be glad to take over—"

Take over, Katherine said to herself. I wonder what he has on the fellow. She wanted to say, "Thanks, no, I'll get along nicely without your indentured servant." But oh, her dress, her perfume, her waiting and longing for this weekend.

Trapped between rebellion and need, she stammered, "That's very nice. I mean . . . it's lovely of you." She couldn't say or ask a thing without giving herself away to listening ears. Not, is he nice, is he a *little* handsome, does he want even a little bit to come or is it straight blackmail? Nothing. Just, "That's lovely."

"You'll like this guy, Katherine. Greg Ferris. A real solid guy." The more Marc spoke, the lower Katherine's heart went. "Well, that's set, then?" Marc sounded amiable now. "Sorry as heck to miss the revels myself, you know."

"You are?" She heard her cold voice and drove warmth into it methodically, as if with a hypodermic needle. "Well, it's very sweet of you to . . . think of it."

"Not at all, not at all. Have to toddle off now and do battle with a book. Oh, yeah, Greg wanted me to ask what color dress you are wearing to the dance on Sat."

"Blue. Light blue." And then she couldn't stand it another second. "Goodbye. It was lovely to hear from you—"

She hung up, stood for a moment staring down at the phone, and turned away. Courage, Katherine, she said soundlessly. Funny how sometimes that did help. Well, she wasn't completely stranded; the weekend wasn't completely lost. Greg Ferris. A real solid guy. She was afraid she knew what that meant. But he'd thought to inquire about her dress.

Please, she prayed, please let him be a little bit handsome, a little bit glad to come.

"Something awry?" said one of the girls, poking her head out of an open door. There were girls behind her, sprawled in chairs, their feet up. A couple of them turned their heads and looked at Katherine questioningly.

"Nothing. He just wanted to know what color dress I'm wearing Saturday night."

She had never mentioned Marc's name, and there was no need for anyone to know Greg Ferris hadn't been her intended date all along. She wondered how she'd have been feeling if she'd described Marc the gorgeous. You didn't need a lot of instinct to know that Greg, his henchman, would not be as gorgeous. You only needed to have read some books.

"Coo," said the girl in the doorway. "Wish somebody'd ask *me* what color dress. I always wind up with red camellias on purple satin."

"The Down East Carmen," said someone behind her. They all laughed, and they did not seem unfriendly, but no one actually asked Katherine in. She bobbed her head at them and went down the hall to her room, closing the door as she always did.

Saturday the girls spent the day getting the house exquisitely in order. They set the tables, arranged flowers, distributed little homemade place cards. Katherine found her own card and Greg's beside it in the center of the long table. It gave her a funny feeling, seeing her name and his written out that way, with little painted nosegays in the corners of the cards. It gave her the most peculiar feeling of mattering.

"Who did these?" she asked a passing girl.

"These? Alice, I suppose. She's the artist around here."

"She got the names from Mrs. Corson, I suppose?"

"I guess."

"They're awfully pretty."

"Oh, sure. Alice is good at that sort of thing. I suspect her of wanting to paint on lampshades." The girl giggled and went on to the kitchen.

Katherine helped arrange the big parlor for dancing. She'd never helped with this sort of thing before, but then she'd never been involved before. It crossed her mind that she might have offered to help anyway. She let this vague thought go unstudied, because there was nothing to do about it now and she didn't have time to be remorseful about things past; she was too worried about things coming. Oh, she was nervous, nervous. . . . She talked and replied and shoved chairs and swept the floor when the rug was rolled and removed, and once in a while she laughed, and she didn't tell a lie all afternoon because no occasion for telling one ever arose.

At the end of their labors the house looked strange and shining and hopeful. She stood in the doorway of the parlor with her fellow workers and looked at the temporary ballroom and found it good. Then they all moved over to the dining room to inspect the long table with its not very good silver and glassware, its very pretty flowered centerpiece. Someone—Alice again, probably—had made a lot of crepe-paper rosettes and had wreathed the chandelier with them.

"Well, I must say," the house president commented, "this room certainly looks girlish."

"Just what the boys will love," Mrs. Corson predicted comfortably. She looked as proud and peaceful as a pigeon on a sunny ledge. "All right, girls, hurry along and start fighting over the bathrooms. You haven't *too* much time."

They trooped upstairs, and Katherine was among the troop, part of it for a while, anyway. After she'd finished her bath and was in her room, with the door closed, she sat down in her slip and looked directly at a notion that had caught in her mind.

Possibly the fact that she was almost always alone was not all their fault. Conceivably her lies and her aloofness, designed at first to show them she was valuable and different and that she didn't care what anyone thought, had simply insulted them. That woman on the train that day had clearly been insulted by her tales of famous friends, of law school and traveling abroad. There was no reason why a girl should not have famous friends, should not become a lawyer or travel alone in Europe, but something in the way Katherine spoke proclaimed the lies, and the woman had been not impressed but offended.

And I knew it at the time, Katherine thought, forgetting to worry about Greg Ferris. I knew it and went right on. Why? She looked at her closed door and then walked slowly over and opened it to look out into the hall. No, not one other door was closed. Girls rushing back and forth, girls' voices pitched high as girls' voices were, a heavy mixture of fragrances in the air. Very much a dance evening in a sorority house. Much borrowing and commenting—and hers the only privacy.

Maybe she could try—oh, openness, instead of falsehoods and seclusion? She could *try*. Self-consciously, she stepped away from the door, leaving it open, and continued dressing. She was spraying perfume on her hair when a figure in flame taffeta appeared at the door.

It was Alice, the artist, who said, "Say, you—" Then she stopped and tipped her head a little. "Very nice. Sort of cinquecento. Most unusual."

Katherine flushed, disproportionately pleased. "You look nice, too," she said promptly.

To herself she sounded too eager, but Alice said casually, "Oh, I'm the Modigliani type, worse luck. Long face. Still, I make do."

Katherine started to quote the famous artist from her town. She knew him as well as she knew the famous author, the famous actor, the famous scientist, which was scarcely at all. A sentence formed in her mind: "And he told me that at the very *first* opportunity I absolutely, positively *must* pose for him."

"The chandelier looks absolutely, positively divine," she said instead, and if her voice was a bit too intense for the matter, Alice apparently didn't notice that either. She looked gratified and said it had taken at *least* as long as a term paper to do. A very long term paper.

"Oh, golly," she said, "I forgot what I came for. Your beau Ferris is downstairs. And coo-*ee*. Are there any more at home like him?"

Katherine's heart lifted. Nice, then? Handsome? It would seem so. Alice would not be easy to impress. The snake's-tongue flicker of suspicion came again. Was this why Alice was so friendly? Greg Ferris was someone they could use around the house, so now they'd be clubby? She stiffened, frowned, and then in a moment made her decision. Okay, maybe that was true. Why not? Everybody had to like somebody for something in the beginning. So, if they wanted to start liking her for Greg, well, she'd just have to try to take it from there. And if that's a homily, she said to herself, let me make the most of it.

There was only one boy in the downstairs hallway. He stood there looking up rather apprehensively, holding a little white florist's box in his big hands. When he saw her, his face—a good, strong, *hewn* sort of face—brightened. Katherine's heart went out to him for that brightness and for the tentative, hopeful way in which he said, "Katherine?"

Oh, Marc, she thought. Oh, my dear, dear cousin Marc. Thank you.

She nodded and went down to Greg.

She skimmed like a deer, swam like a salmon, soared like a swallow through the evening. Through the dinner and the dancing and a lovely long time of sitting on a library window seat, just talking with Greg.

"But how did you happen to come?" she asked daringly. "How did Marc, for heaven's sake, *persuade* you?" She could say something like that, something that did not dignify her or cloak her in mystery, because she felt so happy with him. Who cared about dignity and mystery when a boy's frank admiration shone from his wonderful face?

"Well—" He hesitated, then smiled. That's what roguish means, Katherine decided. He has a roguish smile.

"Well— You aren't gone on Marc or anything awkward like that, are you?"

Katherine shook her head easily. "He's my cousin," she explained, as though that explained all. "I only asked him—" she stopped, then plunged on—"because I didn't know anyone else to ask." No embroideries. No lies. The plain truth.

Then the thing happened that surprised her so she all but laughed. He didn't believe her. Quite clearly, he assumed she was withholding something. His eyes respected her for it. "You're something of a mystery, aren't you?" he said, and Katherine turned away.

"Why *did* you come?" she asked again, when she could control her smile.

"Well, I don't know whether you know this girl of Marc's or not," Greg said. Katherine shook her head. "A mortification to him. Broke off a week before Christmas, gave back his pin. Broke on again the beginning of the week and took the pin back. He's afraid to tell her he had another date. Human, all too human."

"I still don't see why you came."

"Oh, that's simple," he said. "I like the guy. Didn't mind helping him out of a spot. He said you were very pretty, and I didn't have anything else to do, so here I am and darned glad of it."

She thought: Are things always this simple when they're true?

When my love swears that she is made of truth . . .

What she had not noticed—the young English instructor had pointed it out, but Katherine was an expert at not noticing what she preferred not to notice—was that the woman of lies in the sonnet was lying to flatter and warm and protect the man, not to enhance her own value.

It would be better, she said to herself solemnly, to be loved not in spite of things, but for things. She realized what a long time it had taken her to get here.

There was no reason to think that Greg would—or would not—love her, but now she was going to stop lying her way through life. Probably things were not always simple just because they were true, but at least, she thought with a deep sigh, she wouldn't have to remember what she'd said the last time.

"Tired?" Greg asked solicitously.

"No, I feel as if I were just waking up."

"Well, good." As the music from the record player in the parlor began, he got to his feet and held out his hands. "Shall we dance?" he asked her.

A Very
Continental Weekend

*T*here was no privacy anywhere. Not at home, where her parents watched over her with brooding concern (their fledged but unflown chick) and would say, at any suspicion of withdrawal or detachment, "Betty, darling, what is it? Is something wrong? You can tell *us,* you know."

Could she say, "But I cannot tell you, and you can't help me, and I just want to be alone"?

It was out of the question. She and her elderly parents loved each other with that stiff-necked, nervous, uncomprehending love which so often exists between generations and precludes ease of manner or freedom of expression. Besides, they never wanted to be alone themselves, and would not understand why she did.

Certainly if she explained that it was because Chris Brennan was apparently going to stick to his decision (which she hadn't told them about) and not take her out any more, she'd never be let alone. They'd exclaim in outrage and indignation. They'd run him down as wholeheartedly as, in the past two months, they'd run him up.

They'd tell her there were just as good fish in the sea as ever came out of it. They'd try to be with her every possible minute and they'd call her friends to rally round. They'd offer, in abundance, the sort of consolation they felt the situation called for, and never think that it wasn't acceptable.

How could she say, "Please, please . . . leave me alone. I don't want to be consoled, I just want to be by myself"?

Plainly, she could not.

"How's Chris?" her mother had asked a few nights ago. "You seeing him this weekend? Such a nice young fellow. In some men, you'd say almost too good-looking, but he isn't the sort to get carried away by his own good looks. He's got this modesty, hasn't he?"

Stifling a wish to cry out in protest, Betty agreed that Chris had this modesty. She avoided a direct answer about the weekend. What could she have told them? That after dating her for several successive Saturdays, Chris had said to her last weekend that he found himself getting dangerously fond of her and therefore had decided to stop seeing her (outside the office, where it was frequently unavoidable).

"Forever?" she'd blurted, hurt and not able to understand what she'd done or not done to cause this. They'd seemed to be having such fun together.

"I don't know," he'd admitted. "I just don't know. You see, Betty, I'm not in a position yet to get too fond of any girl." He thought that over and went on with desperate candor, "I don't even *want* to. I mean, sure, in time . . .

only not just yet. You do see, don't you?"

She seized on his tone of anxiety and told herself he couldn't care so much that she understand if he did not care very much for her, that what he was saying was not just a kindly excuse to stop seeing a girl in whom he'd lost interest, but a literal statement of fact. If, indeed, he was dangerously fond of her, would a refusal to see her put an end to it? Rather the reverse, if you could believe books and adages.

While she was still with him that evening, she managed to be controlled, even gracious. She wanted to shriek at him, to ask how he thought he could engage someone's heart this way and walk off with a casual "Sorry," how he presumed to tell her in all but words that she was to wait and hope but he wasn't making any promises. But she kept her voice gentle and said yes, she did understand how a man might feel that way, and for that matter she wasn't entirely sure herself that she wanted to limit her attention to just one man.

Had he picked up his ears rather sharply at that? Had an expression of doubt entered the stream of self-justification? She couldn't be sure. Wanting to finish the evening and leave with him, intact, the picture of a girl a man might well wish to return to, she had time only for self-observation. It was watch each word, guard each glance, prevent at all costs the emergence of a girl who lay just under the surface quivering with outrage, a girl who felt entitled to a scene and might at any moment, regardless of the consequences, throw it.

She'd made it safely to the door, and, as if fate now and then relented when she'd pushed you to the breaking point, her mother and father had already gone to bed when she let herself in. So she was able to steal to her room unobserved and cry half the night unconsoled. It had done her some good. It left her still with her parents to face morning and evening, the office to face all day from Monday to Friday without, now, the happy feeling rising on Thursday morning that any moment he would come to her and say, "Doing anything Saturday, Betty?" He'd never been more definite than that, had never said, at the close of one Saturday evening, that he'd like to see her the next. He had never suggested a date during the week, and Betty, loving Saturdays, had schooled herself not to ask (though she had to wonder) what he did with the other six evenings.

But twice in the past month she had made up her mind that *this* Thursday when he came to her desk as if by accident and asked, as if only remotely concerned, whether she were busy Saturday, she would say, "Sorry, I've a date that night. How about some other time?" She told herself sternly that she offered no challenge, turning into a happy limpet and saying, "No, no, I'm not busy at all," practically before he'd put his question. You had to pique a man, tempt him with uncertainty, lead him this way and that. Anyone knew that. Certainly Betty Rowan, a girl well dated from the age of fourteen through high school and two years of college, knew it.

Betty Rowan had never been in love before. She

was pretty sure she was in love now. It made a terrible difference. Easy enough to pique, tempt and mislead a man if you didn't basically care whether he asked you again or not, but love, it appeared, made you a coward. You simply could not risk having him say indifferently, "Oh, that's too bad," and then not follow it up with any suggestion at all.

Well, her tactics, if tactics you could call them, had been wrong, but if Chris was to be believed, no others would have served her better. He simply wasn't going to get seriously involved with anyone. Betty tried to believe this, but a small sad voice informed her that no man decided when to fall in love. If he'd been going to love her, he wouldn't have been able to make a cool prudent decision to stop before he did.

And that, she told herself, as the intolerable Thursday morning passed with no sign of Chris, who worked in the layout department two floors above, is what I have to face. He was letting me down kindly.

Kindly was a word like a mallet splintering her reserve, and she wanted to cry out against it, as she'd wanted that night to shriek at Chris. It was quite terrifying, this fear that suddenly, in the full view of the office, she would let out a demonic yell or burst into wild sobbing.

And there really was no privacy anywhere.

She went from her desk to the file cabinet with a sheaf of folders and began, with glazed eyes and clumsy fingers, to tuck them away, checking and rechecking for accuracy. I must not make mistakes, she reminded herself over and over. My job is my job, not my love life. Somewhere, sometime, I liked this job, and sometime I'll like it again. I must not let it suffer because I am suffering.

She wished that it were possible to leave it, just for today. Only where would she go if she pleaded sudden illness? Home? That would be worse than staying here. Last night she had told her parents that she and Chris were not seeing one another any more, trying to make it sound a mutual decision. They knew her too well and had guessed the truth immediately. With a peculiar disregard of what she might be feeling, they'd proceeded to take out their anger for her in abuse of Chris. She did not want Chris abused. She only wanted not to talk about him, and they wouldn't see it. No, she couldn't go home. She supposed she could ride around on a bus or something, but what was to keep her from crying on the bus? The truth was, an alteration in routine was beyond her and she felt physically able only to stay here or go home.

There's nowhere, nowhere, she thought over and over. I'm like that woman in the Katherine Mansfield story, I want to cry and can't think of anywhere to go and get on with it. What she wanted to do was lean her arms on the file cabinet and weep for hours. She wanted not only to weep into the files, she wanted to crawl into them. She wanted to crawl into some corner of her own mind and die there for a while and be aware of nothing.

She filed away the folders as she had to, neatly and correctly and carefully, and then, as she had to, neatly closed the drawer and returned to her desk, which was one of several in the office adjoining the editor's and left her open to the gaze of eyes right, left and behind. Of eyes ahead, too, should anyone care to turn and study her, though everyone seemed intent on his work.

During her absence at the file cabinet, two manuscripts had been left on her desk for reading. Usually this gave her a sense of exhilaration, of moving forward in the wonderful world of publishing. She was, actually, a clerk, but from time to time the editor allowed her to read and comment on manuscripts. In time, with enthusiasm and taste —she had both—she'd get to be a reader. Until Chris Brennan had come down that day from the layout department and spied her and put his casual request for a Saturday-evening date, it was all she'd been concentrating on.

Oh, but I was happy then, she mourned. Just a little over two months ago, and I was so free, so happy, so full of confidence and hopefulness, in such absolutely charming proportions, if I'd only known it. Her father said nobody recognized happiness except in retrospect, but Betty didn't believe him. She didn't believe him even now. How about all those Saturday evenings with Chris? She'd been transcendently happy, and aware of it, and grateful for the awareness. All except the last one. Nobody ever claimed that people didn't recognize unhappiness when they had it. Nobody could. Unhappiness hit you in the eye, hit you in the heart, made itself felt.

She pulled one of the manuscripts toward her, reminding herself that well-bred people did not make scenes of grief in public. What in the world do well-bred people do?

she wondered a bit wildly. She caught her lower lip, which breeding could not keep steady, and breathed deeply, and ran some paper into her typewriter.

"Something wrong, Betty?" the woman at the desk to her right, secretary to the editor, inquired softly.

Betty shook her head, frantic at the kindly tone. Kindness now would be her undoing. She took another deep breath, managed to say, "Nothing, really," managed, even, half a smile, though keeping her eyes averted.

The woman either believed her or understood. She nodded and resumed her typing.

That was really the worst part of a next to unendurable morning. Noon came and brought no sign of Chris, but did bring some peculiar sort of letdown that made her emotions more manageable. She was not afraid now that she'd cry, and the afternoon would be somehow got through, and tomorrow would. She'd passed a crisis, and here she was at the other side of it, emptied of hope or pleasure, but repossessed, in a tired way, of her reason.

Reason is not the most dazzling faculty, but its return is reassuring to people who've been badly shaken by emotion. Reason now suggested that she was a grown person, taking her chances in the field of love, and if she'd had a fall, she had a right to be hurt but no right to be outraged.

If I could only be alone, she thought over and over, I could somehow find a way of believing in my reason rather than my heart, which goes right on being miserable in spite of logic.

It was after lunch, when she was rereading the manuscript she'd read that morning with no comprehension at all, that Lisa Bergholt, a Danish girl who had a position similar to hers, came across the office to sit on the edge of her desk and make the, to Betty, completely astounding proposal that she buy a railroad ticket and a reservation at a New England inn for the weekend.

"Buy them?" Betty said blankly. "Buy them from whom? I mean, what for?"

"From me," said Lisa in what Betty always thought of as her blonde accent. Lisa was the blondest person Betty had ever seen. Not precisely pretty, but rather devastatingly showy. And just as bright as she was blonde. Every time Chris came into the office, Betty wanted to throw a bag over Lisa's head, or a smoke-screen over that end of the room, to keep him from seeing her, though he apparently never had.

Apparently was not a reliable word.

"I was," Lisa explained easily, "going off this weekend for a little time by myself. Sometimes I think that if I don't see a tree or smell some air that doesn't come out of the back of a bus, I'll lose my mind. So off I go. This weekend, this is where I was going, to this little inn in your beautiful New England."

"All by yourself?" Betty said. Lisa was probably her own age, slightly past twenty. The idea of a girl's going off all by herself this way was astonishing, and Betty tried to think what her parents would say. Lisa, she'd heard somewhere, was staying here in the United States with an American aunt and uncle. An aunt and uncle, acting *in loco parentis,* would surely find this a questionable, possibly even dangerous venture? She said this to Lisa, who laughed a rich, blonde laugh.

"Certainly not," she said. "They understand that anyone needs privacy sometimes. Even young people. Though here in America one wonders that they need it as little as they do."

Betty stiffened slightly. "Everybody needs privacy." Some people certainly can't find it, she thought. "It isn't a purely European requirement. But going off alone at your —I mean, at our—age. It just seems funny."

"Not in Europe," Lisa said calmly. "We take these things differently, I expect. This is a very Danish—a very continental—thing to do. Young girls in Denmark have to go by themselves once in a while and think. The same as the young men. Don't you think it's odd . . . America is the most youth-conscious country in the world—you find it so, do you not?—and yet here is this tremendously important aspect of human life, of young lives, that you neglect altogether. The need of a person to be alone, to think, to be by *himself* from time to time. Your young people act as if they're scared to be by themselves. Why do you suppose this is?"

"You tell me," Betty said grimly.

"I suppose—" Lisa began, and broke off, as if conscious for the first time that she was on delicate ground. High on brains and vocabulary, Betty thought, but low on sensibility. Yet it was difficult to take offense at Lisa's frequent comments on the American scene. Perhaps because she was so detached. Her remarks were scarcely ever personal, and she never seemed to be discussing herself or yourself. She was concerned with types.

"No, go on," Betty said. "I'm interested."

She was. She'd found that one way to forget—momentarily—a personal hurt was to become involved in an objective interest. The sad truth was that large perspectives rarely won out over subjective preoccupations, but they did provide a sort of delaying time. In the broad daylight of human concern your small private pain was vanquished (though you could rely on it, like a sneak thief, to return with the dark).

"Why do you think we're afraid to be by ourselves?"

"Oh, I don't mean you," Lisa said. "I don't know enough about you to say. But—generally speaking—you know ... American young people go in clusters. Of course, sometimes it's a cluster of two—can you have a cluster of just two?"

"I don't think so," Betty said. "Two is a brace."

"Well ... but you see what I mean? Never alone."

"I see what you mean. I'd like to hear what you think is the reason."

Lisa debated. "Well, hoping you won't take offense," she began, in a tone that clearly said she didn't care one way or another, being too interested in the pursuit of knowledge to allow any danger of personal offense to hinder her, "I can't help but think it's because you—not, you comprehend, you yourself, but you collectively—are afraid that if you get alone you won't find anybody there.

That is to say, you exist only in relation to other people, and the more people, the more you exist." She looked at Betty happily, as if they'd arrived at a scientific truth.

Betty, torn between laughter, outrage and a lurking suspicion that there was something in this analysis you couldn't entirely discard, cast about in her mind for an answer. As a representative of American youth, she must not allow this Danish challenger to unhorse her at the first thrust. On the other hand, aside from a certain weak protest that generalities were never accurate (the trouble was, they often were), she couldn't think of a ready refutation.

She could not, at the moment, call to mind any young Americans of her acquaintance who wanted to go away and think by themselves. She herself wanted most desperately to be alone for a while, but that was to lick a wound and wasn't what Lisa had in mind at all. When I'm happy, Betty thought, or just not unhappy, I rarely crave privacy. The fact was, she liked being with other people, and so did practically everyone she knew. In college there'd been an odd (really odd) person here and there who demanded privacy. If she remembered correctly, the result was they got nothing but. A genuine nonconformist (not the ubiquitous sort you found nowadays who got together with a huge band of his fellows and followed a rigid pattern of nonconformity) was rare and, for purposes of this argument, useless. Besides, it appeared that in Europe—anyway in Scandinavia—there was nothing in the least unusual in a young person's going off by himself to think it all over, so there'd be no credit in claiming that she knew a few people who did.

But what's the matter with us, she wondered, that we *don't* want the . . . the replenishment that time by ourselves could offer?

Would I like to take this ticket and reservation from Lisa? she asked herself. It would be a very strange, unexpected thing to do, to go off by herself to an unknown place for the weekend. It would give her that time alone she'd been so much needing. What in the world could she tell her parents? To go away for a couple of days with another girl—that they would understand perfectly. They would send her off with their blessing, a bit of extra money and a lot of weatherwise suggestions. But alone? Maybe she could go without telling them the precise circumstances. This thought entered her mind and flowed right through. She didn't lie to her parents. She didn't, if she could help it, lie to anyone. It tended to upset her stomach. Very well, then, if she took this ticket, etc., she would have to face her parents and confess to them that she wanted, enough to do a very peculiar thing, some time away from them. It would not be at all easy.

"I don't know," she said to Lisa.

"Know what?" said Lisa, who'd picked up the manuscript Betty had been reading. "What part of the conversation are we on? This story has some real graces, don't you think?"

Betty, despite heartache and indecision, was drawn into a discussion of the story. It was a quality that would one day make her a good editor, and only when Lisa glanced at the clock and said she'd better be getting back to her desk did they remember the purpose of her being here to begin with.

"Why aren't you going off for the weekend yourself?" Betty asked.

"Oh, that's because I got invited to a typical American festivity—activity? What would you call a football game?"

"Organized murder, but then I don't have the typical American attitude toward it," Betty said, and smiled at herself for sounding a little proud of being different. Lisa had that effect on people.

"So . . . that's very interesting," Lisa said seriously. "Still, I must experience all that I can. And Christopher Brennan—you know him? From the layout department? —he asked me to go to a football game this weekend up in Yale, which is where he went to school. I think this is a chance I shouldn't miss. To go to a typical American sport with this so very American young man. Don't you agree?"

"I think you're bearing down a bit on that typical."

My face, she told herself, is a mask. Lisa won't guess what I feel. She isn't even responsible, except indirectly. Even Chris isn't responsible. I took my chances in love, the same as everyone else, and I lost, and I honestly don't think I'm complaining—much. I just want to be alone for a while to catch my breath.

"Am I?" said Lisa thoughtfully. "Yes, I guess I am. I get carried away by the investigative process."

I wish you'd get carried away by a disintegrating process, Betty thought, not entirely meaning it. There was that in Lisa which no one, not even a wounded and undeclared rival, could dislike. A sort of openness. Which is not, Betty told herself somewhat aggressively, typically anything. Danish, American or Afro-Swiss. It was just a quality some people had.

"Do Danish girls," she said slowly, "go off on these solo weekends to recover from . . . blighted romance, as it were?"

"Oh, my, yes. It's a specific, practically. At such times you need a bit of everything. A little understanding consolation from your friends, a little standing-by on the part of your family—" Lisa ticked these items off on her fingers in an experienced way "—but mostly and above all you require perspective. You must get away from the round track that constitutes your daily pattern. Now, think it over, Betty," she went on in a spirited way. "You get up every day in the same room, eat with the same morning people, probably the same sort of meal. You come to work by the same route, undoubtedly. Do you alter your route much? Take a different transportation, walk instead of riding?"

Betty shook her head, mesmerized. She came to the office from her home in New Jersey by bus and subway, and it never occurred to her to alter either morning or evening routine.

"So . . . you see?" Lisa said with an air of triumph. "Now then . . . you get to the office, where your desk is always in the same place, and do interesting but similar work—similar, that is, to the work you've done the day before, and the day before that—and you go to lunch with the same people at a choice of the same few places, and then you go home and it all begins again. See what I mean? The result is you can't help but get your perspective narrowed. Not narrow, necessarily. But narrowed. Funneled down. And the person you adore . . . you do adore him?"

"I don't know," Betty said, faintly uncomfortable, but not sufficiently to protect or break up the conversation. It was like talking with a young professor of the heart. Lisa sounded so absolutely competent and sure of her subject. "I guess I wouldn't call it adore. I *think* I love him."

"Even more painful," Lisa said soberly. "This person you love, or think you love—it comes to much the same thing while you're feeling it, except that if you can say *think* it's possible you're getting over it— Where was I? Oh, yes . . . after a while you develop a—what shall I say? What was that good expression I heard the other night? Ah, yes—you develop a sort of *rifle vision* about this person. You know what this is, this rifle vision? It's a straightly directed stare that cannot take into account anything to one side, or above, or below. It concentrates on one object. Now, is it any wonder you get to believing that object to be the only one on the scene? When this happens to me, I go off somewhere to broaden my view. Your own poet, your perfectly glorious Edna Millay, has written a charming verse on the matter. Do you know it?"

"I'm not sure," Betty said, thinking that, compared to this girl, she was like a child. Do people grow up quicker in Denmark, she wondered, or am I retarded?

Lisa, her head back, was reciting with every evidence of delight,

" 'The fabric of my faithful love
    No power shall dim or ravel
Whilst I stay here,—but oh, my dear,
    If I should ever travel!' "

Betty smiled, and Lisa said, "Written to order, is it not? Oh, yes, I have had such lonely, restorative weekends."

"Often?" Betty said diffidently.

"Countless times," said the Danish girl. "I am ruled by the heart. Or some such organ," she added thoughtfully.

Betty could think of no reply to that, but she said, not allowing time for further reflection, "All right. How much will this restorative, broadening weekend set me back?"

"You're laughing at me?" said Lisa cheerfully. "Well, that's all right. You'll find I'm right. I'm not guaranteeing you'll get over the man, mind. But, on my *troth,* you'll see him in a less tortured light. What more could a woman ask? Except the man himself, of course, and in the long run that might not be the best answer, don't you agree?"

Feeling deluged with words, oddly a bit comforted, resentful of Lisa and grateful to her, Betty merely shook her head. Oh, well, she thought. I'm not the first person to be somewhat charmed by the enemy. Look at Queen Elizabeth and Mary of Scotland. Look at Caesar and the treacherous Cleopatra. Look at Louis XIV, and the Duchess of Burgundy. He knew she was sending French secrets to her Savoyard father, and still he couldn't resist her. It's not always as simple as saying, That person's on the other side from me and therefore I'll dislike him. With these lofty, farfetched examples in mind, she looked at Lisa and said, "I really have to thank you. . . ."

After dinner that evening she said to her parents in an overstern voice that she was going away for the weekend.

"Well, darling," said her mother. "You don't have to sound so defensive about it. I think it's an excellent notion. Especially since that . . . since you . . ."

"No point beating about the bush," said Mr. Rowan. "You mean since that Brennan character turned out to have none." He looked pleased with this turn of phrase, and Mrs. Rowan's faint smile congratulated him. "The fact is," he went on with dispassionate interest, "from the outset I was not quite sure of him. I believe you felt the same, did you not?" he inquired of his wife, who nodded thoughtfully and said, all things considered, she had.

Less than a week ago they couldn't praise him too highly, Betty thought, and reminded herself that this was protectiveness on their part.

"On the whole, it's probably for the best," Mr. Rowan went on meditatively, and Betty said to herself, I'm all they have. I mustn't forget that. They just don't know how they sound.

A Very Continental Weekend

Long ago it had taken a family conclave to decide when and where she should go to camp, who was and who was not suitable as a friend, what was to be her choice of a career. Until recently the three of them had even consulted about her clothes, she and her mother shopping and gravely bringing home a selection for Mr. Rowan to study with them. When she left college—a tripartite decision with a foregone conclusion, since they'd run out of tuition money—Betty had decided it was time to stand out for a few other freedoms. At the cost of several painful discussions, she made them see that her wardrobe, the money she retained after paying the board she insisted on, and her hours were henceforth to be her own responsibility. It had never been a conclusive victory, and spots of mutiny appeared from time to time, in her father's gentle "Do you really think that shade of red is your best color, dear?" or in her mother's "Funny, I thought I heard the clock strike two when you got in last night. . . ." As politely as possible, Betty would try not to answer them.

They live through me and for me, she thought now, and it isn't their fault or mine. It's our misfortune. She looked at them, a spare, immaculate couple, sitting in their accustomed chairs, their eyes bent on her with loving bewildered affection, and wondered for the thousandth time why they didn't find some interest in life besides herself. Her father had a job in a printing house which he'd held for twenty-five years and to which he never referred. For the past four years her mother had worked as a part-time saleslady in a department store.

When Betty made any attempt to discuss their jobs with them, they consistently moved the conversation to a discussion of hers, saying with what Betty found sad and convincing honesty that they were only interested in what she did.

They aren't even, she thought with helpless despair, very much interested in each other. Her father seemed to feel that the bulk of his paycheck was about the extent of his responsibility to his wife, and Mrs. Rowan looked after her husband rather like a woman minding the neighbor's plants—adequate attention, but no real concern.

What if I said I was leaving them? Betty asked herself. What if I suddenly announced that I'd taken an apartment with another girl, or even—and this was a new idea, sparked, no doubt, by Lisa—that I was taking one by myself? When in the past the notion of moving out had occurred to her, she'd always dismissed it as impossible. Since she'd never be able to bring the move off, mentioning it at all would be a piece of wanton abuse. But the thought was very strong in her now and would not easily be put aside.

She looked around the room, at the good, sturdy furnishings, the precise draperies, the acceptable ornaments. It was all familiar to a point of being unnoticeable, yet tonight she noticed it sharply. Nothing has changed in years, she thought. This room, this house have survived untouched—except to fade a little—since I was a child. It is the house Mother and Dad made for us three a long time ago. Even her own room was a girl's, last changed when her parents redid it as a sixteenth-birthday present for her.

I should like, she thought with a sense of profound surprise, to have an apartment of my own. I'd like to come home evenings to an untidy place full of brilliant colors, with no curtains, and lots of books, and furniture that the cat could scratch. Because I'd have that, too. A little tigerish sort of cat who'd greet me when I came in but wouldn't insist on knowing why I was half an hour late.

"Betty, dear, I don't believe you're paying attention." Mrs. Rowan unexpectedly lifted her voice, and Betty started. "We—your father and I—have been speculating as to where you'll be going this weekend, and with whom."

Betty took a deep breath and said, "To New England. With nobody."

In the silence that followed she had a chance to think that what she really wanted was not an apartment of her own and a tiger cat. What she wanted was a sense of herself as a grown person. If she seemed like a child next to Lisa, it was because in so many ways she lived like one.

"If I heard you correctly," her father was saying, "it's out of the question."

At the same time Mrs. Rowan was blinking rapidly and saying that if Betty thought this amusing, if she considered it humor, then their ideas of humor were certainly very, very different. "We know you're hurt about this young man," she pointed out, "but it's hardly an occasion for wild talk. It's a time to draw closer to the people who love and understand you, not a time to make fun of them."

They're alarmed, Betty thought. Maybe they sense a resistance in me that I've scarcely had time to feel myself. "Mother, please," she said. "And Dad. I'm not trying to be humorous, and at the moment I don't think anything's funny. I bought this train ticket and a reservation to a perfectly respectable little Massachusetts inn, and I'm going there to . . . to be by myself," she ended on a rising note.

"You can be by yourself here," Mrs. Rowan said stiffly. "I'm sure your father and I never want to interfere with you. Why, I never even go in your room without knocking on your door, now do I?"

"Oh, *Mother*. You just don't understand."

"That's what young people always say when they want to do something wrong."

"I don't want to do something wrong. What do you think I'm planning . . . an assignation with the boss?"

"Elizabeth!" said Mr. Rowan, and if Betty hadn't felt so harried, she'd have laughed inwardly. It was his Barrett of Wimpole Street tone, and she hoped he'd never know that it touched her not with awe but with fondness, sadness and an impulse to giggle. They are a Victorian pair of parents, she thought, but I am not a Victorian daughter, and nobody in this household is ever going to understand anybody else.

"Elizabeth, we'll have no such irresponsible *unlady*like talk," Mr. Rowan said, and Mrs. Rowan said perhaps Betty was a bit excited, but of course she must see that they could not allow her to do any such unheard-of thing as traipsing off to New England by herself, and did she really think Christopher Brennan worthy of such melodramatics?

Goaded out of patience, Betty stamped her foot and said, "Listen to me, I am twenty-one years old!" And then she did laugh, because it was all so ludicrous. You could stamp your foot and say you were ten years old, or maybe even fourteen years old. But to stamp it and announce that you were twenty-one? It was too nonsensical. She dropped into a chair and pushed her hair back and wondered if everybody had this much trouble with parents.

"You aren't twenty-one yet," said Mrs. Rowan. "Not till November."

Mr. Rowan said what did age have to do with it anyway? The question was one of propriety.

Oh, lord, thought Betty. Nothing will ever change. I can hear them saying in years to come, "Betty is a very young thirty-five. Betty is an immature forty-eight," and I'll still be living here and they'll still be living through me, and I just cannot *allow* it.

With a sense of now or never, she leaned forward and said, "Mother and Father, please listen to me, because what I have to say is very important to all of us and you aren't going to agree with any of it and I'm not going to change my mind."

They looked so stunned and apprehensive, so quickly uncertain of themselves, that she almost relented, almost decided nothing was worth the bother and the hurt, not what she'd have in mind to say, not the weekend, not anything. Let's just let everything go on as before, she was about to say, when Mrs. Rowan said, "I knew that young man was a troublemaker. This is all his fault."

To defend Chris gave Betty a painful sort of comfort and made her resolute where, speaking only for herself, she wouldn't have been.

"Chris isn't at fault anywhere," she said. "Not anywhere. He liked me, and we had some lovely times together, and that was all. If I made . . . something more of it, he's certainly not to blame."

With the rather subtle design of weakening their arguments by arousing their compassion, she let them see more than she'd wanted to how much she had cared for Chris and, even as she did it, felt resentful that she had to. "Look," she said abruptly, "tell me why it is I have to explain myself so thoroughly to my parents at my age. Do you really think that's right? Or dignified?"

The rest of the evening went on like a bad dream, with a good deal of harking back to Betty's childhood when she had loved and trusted and relied on them implicitly, and a lot of protest on her part that she still loved and trusted them but surely even they could see that she wasn't a child any more and must rely on herself.

Her mother wanted to know what she meant by even, and Mr. Rowan reminded her that she was not yet fully of age, and Betty, hardly caring what she said any more, told them that if they didn't stop badgering her she'd move out for good.

This was followed by a long silence. Mrs. Rowan

covered her mouth with her hands and stared blindly across the room. Mr. Rowan knocked out his pipe and refilled it with trembling fingers. Betty rested her head against the back of the chair, feeling shaky and a bit sick. It occurred to her in a distant fashion that she was scarcely having a moment to be heartsick over Chris, thanks to Lisa and her peculiar, timely, explosive suggestion. Probably she should be grateful, but she wasn't. The weekend by herself had far less to do with Christopher Brennan, or even with privacy, than with Betty herself and how her life was to be lived. It certainly no longer seemed a good idea or in the least restorative, and she couldn't help wishing she'd never heard a word about it.

When I am a parent, she thought, listening to the voices of her own parents swirling about her in tones alternately pleading, sarcastic, autocratic and frightened, when I am a parent, please let me remember this night and what brought it into being. Let me remember that my children are not my children. They are life's, or God's, or their own, but they are not mine.

"Stop it!" she cried out suddenly, and jumped to her feet.

"See here, young lady," her father began to bluster, but he broke off and turned away. Mrs. Rowan said nothing. Betty, who had a lot to say, ran a hand through her rumpled hair and let her shoulders slump.

"I guess we'd better go to bed," said Mrs. Rowan then, and on this sad, inconclusive note they parted for the night.

A Very Continental Weekend

Betty lay awake for a long time, thinking about love.

Love, she said to herself. Now, what is love? Love is . . . what?

Love, she thought, as she grew drowsy, is like one of those huge Indian deities—juggernauts? Vishnu?—who sat on their heavy cars and rolled over the idolatrous population, crushing it. She wondered, falling deeper and deeper into sleep, how she could have conceived of it as tender and vital and warm, as human.

In the morning she packed an overnight bag and carried it past the kitchen into the hall. "I guess I'll leave right from the office this afternoon," she said nervously, sitting across from her father in the breakfast nook.

He patted his lips with a napkin, nodded slightly and pretended that only politeness kept him from picking up the morning paper.

"Go ahead and read, Dad," Betty said. "Don't let me disturb you." He never read the paper at breakfast, but apparently there were to be changes made. Now he picked it up and turned to the second-section summary with a purposeful air.

"How would you like your egg?" said Mrs. Rowan at the stove.

"Mother, please," said Betty. "I'm not an overnight guest. You know how I like my egg."

Instead of replying, Mrs. Rowan walked to the kitchen door, studied the bag in the hall for a long moment, returned and put two pieces of bread in the toaster. There were two stiff lines at the side of her mouth that Betty hadn't known to be so deep.

"Please," she said again. "Do we have to be this way? I'm only trying to—to grow up." It sounded childish, put that way, but she persisted, hoping to disperse this almost solidified misery that lay among them, a thing of their own fashioning. "You grew up, didn't you? Both of you? Why shouldn't I? Why should it make a difference in our—" she wanted to say love, but couldn't use the word "—in our feelings for each other?"

"I don't understand your feelings," said Mrs. Rowan. "I don't understand anything. Not anything."

Mr. Rowan said that reading the morning paper became daily more disheartening. "Corruption everywhere," he said coldly. "I believe I shall write an article on the subject. I shall entitle it, 'Should the Wages of Sin Be Cash?'"

Betty smiled. "That's a good title, Dad. Really. I speak as an embryo editor."

They could usually be drawn into a discussion of her work. But not today. Mr. Rowan put the paper aside and said, "I believe the toast is ready."

Forcing herself to finish the egg and one cup of coffee, Betty was free to rise and say, "Goodbye. Sorry for the fuss. Really I am." What little words we use, she thought. What little words for great, big, painful feelings.

"Goodbye," said her parents in polite unison.

People that unhappy should be left alone, Betty thought. There's nothing else to do about them.

She took a cab instead of the subway when she got to

the city, because of the bag. "Do you alter your route much? Take a different transportation?" Lisa, my friend, she thought, you have started up a chain reaction in my life with your Continental-Danish ideas, and where I'll fetch up, the dear only knows.

It had all, since last night, got beyond, or above, or to one side of Christopher Brennan, who rode up in the same crowded elevator with her and did not stir her pulses. It had become a matter of finding whether she was a herd-oriented American girl who couldn't be by herself. A matter of proving to her parents that she could mature and fall heir to certain adult rights without causing an eternal schism between them. A matter—to put it flatly— of growing up. Perhaps I come to this a little late, she said to herself wryly, but better now than even later.

She got off at her floor, aware that Chris had got off just behind her. Hesitating—ought she to turn and speak, or just keep on walking?—she collided with him and he put a hand on her arm to steady her.

"Sorry," he said, looking surprised and disconcerted.

Betty realized that he hadn't noticed her in the elevator. That was an unexpected and rather bitter dose. Didn't he care for me at all? she wondered. Or is it just that he doesn't have a very good memory?

"What's that?" he said, looking down at the little suitcase in her hand.

"Suitcase," she said, her voice a bit strained.

"Oh. Well, I could take it from you. Carry it someplace."

"Oh, no. I've carried it this far. I'm just going to see it to a corner."

"I see."

They stood deadlocked while morning traffic flowed around them, Chris's eyes embarrassed and uneasy, Betty helplessly remembering when those eyes had looked at her with laughter and affection and perhaps some promise for the future.

She wanted to say, "Don't you remember how you looked at me, and liked to, those nights not so long past? Surely you remember, Chris, how you took me to *The Threepenny Opera,* and held my hand, and when they were singing their daft and raggedy wedding song, you turned toward me in the dark and I knew it and turned to you and we kissed. It was the only time you ever kissed me, and surely you can't have forgotten?"

She wanted to say these things, not because of a hope for the future, but because of some loyalty to the past, and while these thoughts went through her mind, and perhaps across her face, Chris's constrained eyes were fixed on hers, asking for release.

What did he come to this floor for? she wondered. To see Lisa, probably. And now he doesn't know how to extricate himself from me, because he's a kind person and feels some responsibility for me that he can avoid as long as he doesn't actually see me.

This realization formed itself and was followed by another, cold perception. Because it was so fresh in her mind, she recalled her parents saying to her in voices raw with pain and appeal, "Don't you remember, Betty . . . ? Oh, Betty, don't you remember how when you were a little girl you loved and needed us? Surely you can't have forgotten what it was like when you needed us so?"

They had thought that by putting it into words they could make her know that need again, could summon up a feeling among them that was part of the past.

This is what people do to each other, she thought. They do it out of need and call it love. Parents, lovers, friends . . .

"Chris," she said abruptly, "I'm willing to stand here all morning, if we have a conversation. But dumb show has never been my strong point."

He looked almost exaggeratedly relieved, gave her a frightening broad grin and went through the exit door on his way upstairs, forgetful, apparently, of anything he'd come for.

Betty walked slowly to her desk and sat down to muse.

So far as getting perspective on Chris was concerned, she might just as well go home tonight. She'd got it. She'd no longer bend the glare of her rifle vision upon him, because it was not kind. Because—more truthfully—she no longer found him that absorbing. She felt an almost absent-minded twinge of sadness for something lost that might have been lovely, but she had no doubt that something just as lovely would take its place in time.

No, the defection of Christopher Brennan was not the problem. He had just served to bring it into focus. The problem was how to grow up and away from her parents, without hurting them. Well, without hurting them too much. Going away for one weekend wouldn't do it, though as a first flight it might prepare them for another, longer flight. *Anything fledged, flies,* she said to herself. It's a law of nature. She could only hope her mother and father would see that in leaving their house she did not necessarily leave them. Perhaps without her to concentrate on they'd begin to concentrate on one another. It was the sort of thing you were allowed to hope.

How peculiar life was—how sad, how exciting, how unfair, how delicious, how mysterious, how—how many contradictory things all at once. She thought she ought to feel sorry, but the truth was she felt sort of exhilarated. Half closing her eyes, she said without asking herself what she meant, "I'm ready—"

Lisa Bergholt, going by, said in a tone almost reproachful, "For a lovelorn girl, you're looking pretty well self-satisfied."

Betty's eyes flew open. "Am I?" she said, and then, "Well . . . I guess I decided I wasn't in love with him, after all."

"American girls," said Lisa, in her most sweeping fashion, "*never* know what they want. Not ever."

Betty, about to protest, decided she owed Lisa a never-to-be-acknowledged debt, so she smiled and let that pass, thereby proving, in one instance anyway, to be a good deal more grown-up than she knew.